Pride Publishing books by R.A. Padmos:

Unspoken

I0542137

UNSPOKEN

R.A. PADMOS

Unspoken
ISBN # 978-1-78651-937-5
©Copyright R.A. Padmos 2016
Cover Art by Posh Gosh ©Copyright March 2016
Interior text design by Claire Siemaszkiewicz
Pride Publishing

Published in 2016 by Pride Publishing, Newland House, The Point, Weaver Road, Lincoln, LN6 3QN, United Kingdom.

Pride Publishing is an imprint of Totally Entwined Group Limited.

UNSPOKEN

Chapter One

"Hey, shuffle along, will you?"

Stefan looked over his shoulder, right into the somewhat annoyed face of a young man, and mumbled an apology. "You have any idea what time it is?"

The young man took out a cheap-looking pocket watch. "A quarter past ten."

It was an ordinary day in September, 1935, in a Dutch city that could be any Dutch city. Someone was waiting behind him in line at the unemployment office to get the first control stamp of the day. Stefan had no idea his whole life had changed during the few seconds it took to ask an inconsequential question.

He got his stamp, checked carefully when he was due for the next one and only realized why he waited those few seconds extra before he stepped outside when he saw the owner of the pocket watch.

Not a word was spoken about it. He simply walked next to the man whose name he didn't even know, through the streets of their home town, not paying any attention to the all-too-familiar red brick three and four-story houses with their green and brown-painted doors.

"I don't think we've ever met," the man walking alongside him said. "I'm Adri Heyman. Officially painter and plasterer, but you know how much that's worth these days."

"About as much as being a carpenter, I bet. Stefan Doffer's the name." He was half aware of the tightening deep and low in his belly, of the beginning of an erection pushing against the fly of his clean but worn corduroy trousers. Only now Marije entered the corner of his thoughts, her voice warning him it was the dangerous time of the month.

Stefan shrugged. "I live close by, just a few minutes' walk from here. Why don't we see if my wife has a cup of coffee left for us in the pot, before we join the next queue of a few hundred men all wanting the same job?"

Day after day he stood in line, waiting for the next stamp on a piece of paper as proof that he deserved the twelve guilders which would be put into his outstretched hand once a week, like he was begging for alms. And wasn't that exactly what he was doing? He had watched seasons changing into other seasons, seen his eldest child go from newborn to toddler to schoolchild. He no longer tried to understand why there was no demand for his craftsmanship and willingness to work hard for anyone who would give him an honest job for more than the weekly pittance that kept his family from starving right away.

How resigned to the hopelessness of reality he had become! On some days, he knew the only thing that kept him from complete desperation and giving up altogether was the deep-seated feeling of duty concerning his family. No despondency had yet prevented him from spending most of his days looking for work — any kind of work — so that he could hold on to the remains of his pride as a husband and provider, but for how much longer?

"We're there." He took out the front door key to the upstairs apartment, a rather fancy name for three small rooms and an even smaller kitchen. The family shared the attic with the elderly couple who lived one floor above them, but their neighbors kept pretty much to themselves and apart from occasional small talk, Stefan saw or heard little of them. The neighborhood of houses built for skilled laborers and lower rank civil servants was decent enough, with poverty safely hidden behind a façade of weekly scrubbed pavements and shiny polished doorknobs. They paid the rent on time, even if it sometimes meant going without a decent, warm meal for a couple of days because they were clean out of gas tokens, and the man collecting the funeral insurance got his money before anyone else.

Stefan had invited the man to his home because he knew with absolute certainty Adri would find nothing there any married man should be ashamed of. Marije kept a scrupulously clean house, fighting her own private war against slow decline. He wasn't surprised when she greeted the unexpected guest with an outstretched hand and an open smile.

Selle, aged four, and three-year-old Wilfred stared with wide-eyed curiosity at the strange gentleman who had followed their dad up the stairs, while their mum poured out three cups of real coffee and two beakers of buttermilk. Stefan knew the eldest of the two would be bragging to his big sister, as soon as she came home from school, that he had shaken the hand of a new someone she hadn't even met yet. It almost made up for the long wait before he would be old enough for kindergarten.

"We don't get many visitors, except for their uncles and aunts and grannies, of course," Marije explained.

"I'm not intruding on your daily routine, I hope?" apologized Adri.

Stefan knew his wife's reaction before she started the first word. "A housewife who can't find the time to sit down for a cup of coffee isn't worth her title." Still, the house was her domain and he was surprised he had made the invitation to Adri without giving it a moment's thought. It was definitely not like him.

"You met Stefan while looking for a job?" Marije poured out a second cup of coffee.

Stefan avoided Adri's gaze, as if he were being accused of a crime he had yet to commit. "He's a house painter. I'm a carpenter. You're bound to see the same faces over and over again."

He trusted blindly that within minutes Marije could make anyone feel at home. And, soon enough, Adri was telling tall stories about his landlady.

Half an hour later, they walked to the first business that was rumored to be needing someone for a cleaning job.

"You are incredibly lucky, having a wife like that." Adri told Stefan what Stefan had known for years.

There wasn't a job to be had. And for the first time in months, he hardly cared.

* * * *

Marije had done the last round to see if the children were still safely tucked in their beds. She had put her dress and stockings neatly over the back of the chair, had put on her cotton nightdress and slipped into bed beside Stefan. She leaned toward him to kiss him good night. He kissed her back, holding on just a little longer, a little tighter.

"Don't." Her voice contained a gentle but absolute warning. A fourth child would only push them further over the edge into poverty. Was he really prepared to do such a thing for a few minutes of fulfilling a primitive need?

"You don't trust me to be careful? Or should I make do with a hanky, while you turn your face away and pretend nothing is happening? I'm a healthy man, Marije. I'm married. I have my rights."

Marije looked at him with concerned, uncomprehending eyes. Never before had he insisted on his rights as a married man when she'd indicated it was too dangerous, always accepting her female knowledge concerning the whole matter.

She stood up from the bed again to get a towel from the well-stocked linen-cupboard, a silent reminder of better times. "I won't change the sheets before next Monday..." The reproach wasn't even subtle. She took off her knickers and turned on her back, the towel under her lower body. Then she covered them both with the sheet and blankets again.

Stefan unbuttoned the fly of his pajama trousers, not understanding why he could be this turned on. He pushed up her nightdress, waited until she opened her legs and knelt between her thighs. He tried to kiss her, but she turned her head away.

"I'll be extra careful." It was a feeble gesture to make amends and she was right to ignore it.

The erection in his hand seemed almost alive with aggressive need, full and heavy and so hard it actually hurt. Never during his marriage had it been like this, and he closed his eyes in shame while he pushed inside her. He started to thrust, accepting the primal moves as if he were nothing but a rutting street dog that knew only its own pleasure. He forced himself to think about Marije, about his wife, about her full breasts and soft curves, as if she didn't deny herself the best parts of their daily meals so that the little ones never had to go without. He tried to concentrate on the wet heat around his penis, but it was all in vain.

The image of another body forced itself into his thoughts—a male body, muscled and strong. The hands of a man touched him intimately. He moaned, forgetting about the three children in their beds. Forgetting about the child that shouldn't be.

* * * *

The next morning he got out of bed with more enthusiasm than he had felt in a long time, despite lingering embarrassment about his behavior the night before. If a random stranger were to tell him he would find a job for at least a year, today he would believe it blindly. He shaved with more care than usual and made sure his clothes were immaculate. He even remembered to brush his teeth.

To his relief, Marije, though perhaps not yet fully forgiving him, at least looked as if she accepted that, whatever happened, it happened for a reason, and there wasn't much to be done about it. He knew better than to pull her close to make up with her, but she answered his apologetic smile and he decided to count his blessings.

He whistled a happy tune when he walked through the streets, the park and more streets to the building where he would get his control stamp, but stranger than anything was the fluttering and crawling of a thousand insects right in the center of his belly as soon as he noticed the young man he had met only yesterday standing in the queue. It was almost Adri's turn to enter the building, and he didn't see Stefan.

He hadn't been this cheerful—or perhaps he should even call it elated—since forever, but also never before had he been so aware of the threat he was walking right into because he simply had no idea of what was happening to him and why.

After he got the stamp, he hesitated to go straight home. His breathing caught when Adri stood before him. "Coffee and look for work?"

He heard the footsteps next to him, heard the voice telling him about the latest rumors that a contractor was hiring. Sometimes he looked sideways at the man and mumbled a reaction. The sun was shining, there was a gentle breeze and for a short few minutes, he was fully at peace with his existence.

Chapter Two

They had made a habit of waiting for each other after getting their stamp, and after a few days, it was as if it had always been this way—the control stamps, the looking for work, the cups of coffee at Stefan's home and the hand-rolled cigarettes they shared.

Four weeks had gone by but that was just time, and Stefan didn't think much about how easily the days and weeks had passed. That night was no different from so many other nights. They had strolled through the neighborhood before it was time for Adri to go home. It didn't mean anything that Stefan dropped his keys when he wanted to open the front door. It was only logical that they reached out at the same time to retrieve the fallen object and, when their hands touched, it was fully by accident. And yet, for a few seconds that must have lasted an eternity, they were frozen in the shock of recognition—until Stefan quickly grabbed the keys and stood upright again.

"It's me, girl," he called upstairs to Marije, because that was what he always did. He knew he was supposed to double-lock the door for the night, but somehow he had forgotten even this simple routine. The touch of Adri's fingers had burned a sign into his hand. Not until there was a knock on the door was he able to move again, and before he could say anything, the man was inside with him. In the dark, cramped entry to his home, where his wife was waiting upstairs for him to kiss his children good night, he was being kissed by a man.

"Oh God... Oh God... What did I do...?" Adri sounded as shocked as Stefan felt.

"I don't want to scare my wife and children, so I'll keep my voice down and I won't hit you, but I never want to see you at my door again." Stefan pushed the door open. "Get out."

That night Marije told him she had missed her time of the month.

* * * *

He felt like himself again when he caught Adri's gaze, waiting in line for another job neither of them would get, and turned away. It was easy as anything. A man kissing another man? Why would any normal, healthy bloke want to do such a sickening thing?

He remembered how he had walked through the park last summer, with Marije, during one of those rare moments the kids were all at Grandma's for a few hours in the afternoon. It was almost like it had been when they were engaged and had a bit of money and so much free time on a Sunday they didn't know what to do with it. There had been this man, if you could call it that, dressed just a bit too colorfully and moving in a way that would only look attractive on a young woman. The creature had looked Stefan straight in the eye and winked at him.

"Doesn't it make you sick to the stomach?" he had hissed.

Marije had pulled at his jacket. "Don't say a thing like that. That man surely doesn't mean to hurt us. Perhaps he can't help being that way."

"Why should I have to even see dirt like that in our park? Or are you saying it's normal, for men to be like that?"

"Perhaps not normal, no…" she had admitted, after some hesitation.

"So you're agreeing with me."

"But that's no reason to judge that poor man so harshly. I can't imagine anyone choosing to be that way, to be without a loving family, with no respect from anyone."

"Respect?"

"Please, Stefan, *Opoe* Doffer didn't offer to look after the little ones so that we could have a fight. When was the last time it was just the two of us? Let's enjoy it, yes?"

He left the memories for what they were when he saw Adri walk away without looking over his shoulder even once. He didn't dare move until the man had turned a corner, too afraid he would run after him, too afraid he would be spineless and weak.

No one should misinterpret his situation. He worked hard on the days he had a job, and stood for hours in line to hear, 'Sorry, man, nothing today' only to do the exact same thing the next day and the next. He never neglected any of the tasks at home that a man shouldn't leave to his wife, mother or daughter, and he paid more attention to Selle and Wilfred because Marije was too sick to run after two lively boys. He felt his urges night after night, but he didn't press her to allow him the use of her body. And, when she nodded her consent, he was extra careful with her because of the new child growing inside her—but also for a reason he hardly dared to face.

Chapter Three

Stefan recognized the young man from afar, sitting on a bench in the park, and noticed that he too had been seen. He was anything but a coward, didn't run from anything or anyone, so he sat right next to Adri and rolled a cigarette.

"You have a job?"

"Do I look like I have a job?" Adri shrugged. "You sent me away like a mangy dog."

He needed all of his courage to say the words, but he said them nonetheless. "I panicked."

"Why?"

"You really don't know?"

"It's not about what I know. It's about what you've got to say," Adri bit, every word sounding judgmental, like an accusation, and Stefan couldn't blame him.

He was all too aware that he shouldn't be on that bench, talking with this man, and yet the inner calm that he had lost on the day he had chased Adri away had returned. The days of innocence were over. He couldn't unlearn what he had learned then. "Does it matter what I have to say? You must have known right from the start."

"The start?"

"The queue, when we were waiting for the control stamp. You told me to move on. I asked you about the time and you said quarter past ten. What do you want from me?"

Stefan stood up and walked away, but after only two paces he stopped and turned around. "Since that day, since a quarter past ten, I've been obsessed with you." He tensed up as if he were expecting a fight, as if he wanted to beat the man until everything stopped.

"Today is my twenty-first birthday."

Stefan didn't get the message. He just had admitted to the most shameful thoughts a man could possibly have, and Adri was talking about his birthday? "Well, happy birthday. Do you want me to sing for you?" The anger gave way to the beginning of understanding. "I know exactly when I made the fourth child with my wife."

"That was when I started to count the days until I would be twenty-one. I've been to the bathhouse, had a shave. I'm wearing my Sunday best and I even changed my underwear." Adri stared at his shoes. "Yeah, I polished them too."

"Marije and the kids are at Aunt Neeltje's with *Opoe* Doffer. They won't be home until dinner."

Without looking back, Stefan walked down the path, knowing Adri would follow.

* * * *

Whatever he might have thought during the months that led up to this one Sunday afternoon, half-known and consciously pushed aside, nothing could have prepared him for the weight of the moment. Adri had turned twenty-one and had made his desire known, and Stefan had agreed, knowing full well what he was about to do. Even if the most likely thing happened and the act itself proved to be a failure, he had made his choice. He had nothing left to hide behind. He needed to know if the desire — which had been stretching its claws inside him for so many weeks — was indeed authentic. The miserable knowledge that he was depending on income support and odd jobs was apparently enough to confuse a man who surely hadn't needed any more proof that he was truly a man.

In the tiny living room, next to the table that stood in the middle, Adri reached out to him and both men continued the kiss that had started at the bottom of the stairs. Stefan clutched Adri desperately because of everything he had never known, everything he was about to lose.

With a mixture of energetic determination and awkward shyness, Adri started to unbutton Stefan's shirt. "I want to see you naked," he stated simply.

It was the first time another human being had ever said that to him. After years of marriage and fathering four children, he still couldn't say in honesty that his wife had seen him naked even once. He, in his turn, had never seen his wife fully naked. He had suggested it when they had been just married, but Marije had looked at him as if he had some really strange ideas that had no place in a decent marriage.

So he had to ask, "Why do you want this, right in the middle of the day, when you can see everything?"

"Your wife must have told you a thousand times how attractive you are." Adri looked at him with honest surprise. "From the moment I saw you, I knew I wanted this. I stood behind you in that queue and I was sure. This is the one. Then you turned around and I was lost."

"You're going to get naked too?"

Adri laughed and winked. "Oh yes."

Stefan undressed as quickly as possible, to get it over with, not looking at Adri until they were both fully naked.

Adri smiled. "It's okay if you want to touch me."

Stefan held him close, naked skin under his hands. He pulled the younger man down on the narrow strip of floor between table and sideboard. Never before had he felt another hand on his erect penis. Adri's voice whispered in his ear, "So beautiful."

This time he took the initiative for a kiss, and it was the end of everything he trusted to be safe. He had no idea what to do, how to deal with a body so familiar and yet so new and strange. His erection brushed against Adri's and it was enough to bring the message home. They were two men. He was naked, kissing the mouth of another man. His hands were touching the naked body of another man. The overwhelming lust he felt was for another man.

He thrust blindly against Adri's body, trying to find enough friction to end this unbearable tension that threatened to tear him apart. Adri clutched him in his arms and legs, held him prisoner until he had nothing left to give.

For a couple more minutes he rested in Adri's arms, surrounded by pieces of clothing he didn't have any further use for.

"Redhead," Adri sighed.

* * * *

With a towel in his right hand and a bar of soap in the other, he stepped inside the shower stall. For the price of ten cents he had a quarter of an hour all to himself, so he undressed and tried to get the water as hot as possible. This was his privilege as the head and provider of his family, even if he hadn't had a job for months. Marije and the kids used the zinc tub in the kitchen on Saturday night, while he visited the public bathhouse earlier the same day, so that they all started Sunday nice and clean.

He soaped his body, washed his hair, but the unthinking pleasure of this small luxury he usually experienced was replaced by uneasy wondering about his own body. With methodical precision he explored everything within reach. He noticed straight shoulders and strong arms — some problems with his back, but nothing that kept him from a life full of hard physical labor. He touched the coarse hair on his chest that trailed down in a small trace. The belly was flat but lacked muscular firmness. Despite the daily amount of walking and riding his bicycle, his legs remained somewhat skinny, which he suspected was due to a diet that kept him from starving but could hardly be called proper nourishment for a grown man. It was a miracle how Marije managed to stretch out the gravy of the cheap Sunday beef cuts over most of the week, but the facts remained the same. Boiled potatoes with watered-down gravy and whatever cabbage was in season, with a tiny piece of bacon, if even that, were not enough to ever feel truly sated.

Looking at himself with honest brutality, he had to admit he wasn't as healthy and attractive as one could hope for in better circumstances.

He hesitated before he brought his hands to his genitals. In all honesty, he didn't know what to think about the scrotum and penis. It was all there. It worked as it should work. The regular intercourse he had with his wife and the four resulting pregnancies were proof enough of that.

Yet someone wanted him. A man desired this body, and this unremarkable body wanted that man. Long before he had recognized the conscious thought that his body had told him its desire. He thought he had listened and understood, and thus made the fourth proof of his masculinity, his normality. It hadn't helped him one bit. The body was not to be distracted until he gave in. And now he had given in, and the body refused to be satisfied with that one experience. It still wanted more.

His fingers, having lost all shame, gripped around his member. He shivered under the stream of hot water, closed his eyes and started to stroke until completion.

Someone pounded on the door of the shower stall. "Time's up."

He closed the tap, toweled himself down and got dressed. He was going to meet his lover again.

Chapter Four

They walked, each with their own thoughts, with almost military precision through every section of the park. They had no idea how else to spend their time together.

"You've been to my place. You know everything about my family, but I never hear you about yours. Were you raised in an orphanage? Please tell me about where you come from. I promise not to judge you." Stefan encouraged Adri to talk about his personal background.

"I grew up in a normal family, with a mum and a dad. I never lived in an institution and I managed to stay out of them when I decided to leave home." Adri accepted the gentle invitation.

"Your folks mistreated you? You don't sound or look as if you're from a posh background, so you weren't going to study at university and I don't think you were about to marry. What other reason could anyone have to leave his parents' home if he has a place to sleep and a mother to cook and wash for him?" Stefan personally didn't know anyone who'd left the parental home before marriage, and quite a few who'd grown middle-aged in the same rooms they were born in and simply continued the life they had always lived, even after their parents died. Only a minority could afford higher education and needed to find a room with a landlady, and that was only until they too found someone to marry. Few men lived without family of any sort.

"I had a dad and a mum and a big sister. We were a decent family, like your family and like most families. Then my father died in an accident and a bit more than a year later, another father entered our home. He was a widower with a son." Adri paused to take a pull from the cigarette that Stefan had rolled and lit for him. "I was twelve when that man married my mother. Everything changed from day one. My dad had always been easy-going. He believed that a gentle warning was a better instrument to teach a naughty child than harsh punishment. I guess he knew that nothing hurts more for a child than seeing the disappointment in your dad's eyes when you've done something you really shouldn't. My mother's new husband wasn't like that at all."

Stefan made an encouraging sound.

"Everything was supposed to happen exactly as he wished it to happen and right when he ordered it to happen. And it wasn't only my sister and me that he treated that way. My dad had always trusted the household to my mum, like you do with Marije, not giving her housekeeping money but handing over his full wages every Saturday. After she married that man, my mother had to ask for money for groceries and everything else she needed. And he was never pleased about anything. He always found reason to complain. He called me names when I refused to obey his orders, because he certainly never asked for anything. I was a young boy. I'd lost my dad, and now a stranger was acting as if he could take the place of my father just like that? He found fault with my sister because he thought she didn't earn enough as a housemaid. Mum explained that she worked for a very cultivated family and that way she was learning everything to be a good homemaker. She said that was more important than having a little bit more money right now. You know…things like fine cooking, how to take care of your linen, decent manners? That family was good to her, but he forced her to take a job in the textile factory."

"A pity…"

Adri shrugged. "Mother could do no right in his eyes, if only because she'd brought such lazy, useless and insolent brats into this world. If he was behaving that way deliberately to make sure we left home as soon as possible, he did a perfect job. My sister married a young man she knew from the factory. Later he made promotion and they moved to the other side of the country. I haven't heard from her in years, but from what I understand, she became a real lady."

"And you?"

"That man, who became my stepfather, had a son."

"You just told me. Younger than you?"

"Older by a few years."

"A chip off the old block?"

"Stepfather was penny-wise, or perhaps I should call him stingy." It was obvious to Stefan that Adri was pretending not to have heard his question. "He thought even a few cents for the weekly bathhouse visit was a waste of money. Every Saturday night the tub was put in front of the stove and I waited at the sliding door till it was my turn. Mum had always made sure my sister and I could bath in fresh water until we were old enough to visit the bathhouse for a shower, but my stepdad didn't see the need for that. Not for us. Every week he allowed himself a real bath at the bathhouse, and his son was always first in the tub, even before my sister. I hated having to wait for that cold, gray water. And that continued until just before my seventeenth birthday."

"Don't tell me there were four wage-earning people in your family and you still had to use the tub? As soon as you bring in money, you have the right to a decent shower or bath once a week. Everyone knows that," Stefan interrupted, angry about something that wasn't his business anyway, even if he had known about it when it was actually going on. He wouldn't accept it if another man meddled with the way he chose to run his family, so why should another man think differently?

"He demanded I hand in whatever I had earned every week to the last cent. Mum sometimes gave me a guilder or so, but I felt guilty accepting any money from her because I knew she paid for it with her personal allowance and that wasn't much to begin with. No, if I compare my life in those days with the way you treat your wife and kids, I consider myself lucky to have left home at such a young age," Adri said, with a hint of challenge in his voice.

"Is that the reason you are that way, with your dad dying when you were so young and your stepdad being such a tyrant?" Stefan had asked the question before he had time to think about whether or not he wanted to hear the answer.

"I was sixteen and dreamed about men. I dreamed about my stepbrother, the son of my stepdad. Every night he sat at the table, and he slept in the same room as me. He was there and he was a man. He was twenty and to me he was the pinnacle of manliness. I don't think he cared much for me." Adri paused. "One night we were at home alone because our parents had been invited to an engagement party. He had a bottle of gin and offered me a glass. I'd never tasted a drop of alcohol in my life, and, boy, did it give me some really stupid courage. Nasty stuff, by the way."

Stefan brushed against Adri for a second. He had to touch him. "He was your first?"

"You were my first. I told you that." Adri looked at Stefan and smiled. "You're jealous."

Stefan shrugged. "Just tell me what happened? Please?"

"I told him I dreamed about him, that I couldn't keep my eyes off him when he undressed to go to bed. He laughed at what I said, as if he thought it was somehow funny. In a way it was worse than him being mad at me."

At the corner of a street, Stefan stopped for a moment. "I remember being that age. Being made fun of when you were trying to be serious was the worst feeling."

"Yeah, well, the next morning I woke up with a pounding headache and I thought I'd never stop throwing up. I also discovered father and son had had a talk about what I'd said, and before the day was over, I was out on the street with a suitcase in my hand and a few guilders my mum had secretly hidden in my coat pocket."

"You mean that man didn't see any problem in throwing a seventeen year old onto the street for saying something stupid while drunk?"

"How many fathers do you think wouldn't throw their sons out of their homes for saying what I said?" Adri smiled wryly. "What does it matter? I'm not the first this has happened to, and I won't be the last. I accepted all kinds of odd jobs to get enough money for a meal every day and a place to sleep. The easiest way was suggested to me almost right from the start. There were plenty of gentlemen with a certain taste and enough money who'd be willing to pay nicely for the company of a young guy like me. Then a man called Jo Swart found me. He took me under his wing, found me a job and a room, gave me books to read. He's old enough to be my father, but I would have said yes if he had asked me. Not him, though, he never even suggested it. Thought I should wait for someone I really cared about, because there's enough ugliness in this world as it is. He's such a romantic! And you don't want to know how many times I thought I'd found the right one—until the next right one appeared on the stage. Then my boss told me he no longer had enough orders to keep all his painters and plasterers, and the married men with families needed their jobs the most, so I had to get in line twice a day for my control stamp. Then I knew the waiting was over."

"And your mum?" Stefan asked, a bit too eager to change the subject.

"At first I was angry she'd chosen that man who treated her children like dirt. Then I pitied her, because what else could she have done with two growing children and no money? Finally I missed her and summoned up the courage to pay her a visit. It was the middle of the day but there was no one there, so I asked the neighbors — and they told me she'd been buried the day before."

"God…"

"No father, no mother and a sister who doesn't want to be reminded of her background. Even my aunts and uncles and cousins have all been thoroughly chased away by that man — not that I'd expect them to be welcoming to someone like me. Now you know why I like being at your place so much, and that's not even counting the fact that you're there."

Stefan nodded as a sign he understood completely. "A woman changes a house into a home. And how can anyone's life be truly fulfilled without children?"

Adri shook his head. "I meant to say that I admire the way you and Marije treat one another with respect and warmth. I remember that from my own mum and dad, when I was a child — before everything changed. I feel welcome in your family."

A deep pity filled Stefan. "No family to call your own, playing second fiddle to mine, having an inclination no man would ever choose — you must be so lonely."

Adri brushed his hand over Stefan's arm, despite the absolute rule of being discreet about the true nature of their friendship. "And you? How lonely are you?"

* * * *

Once again they were lying on the floor, body touching body, arms and legs clutching in desperation.

"Do with me like you do with your wife," Adri whispered in his ear.

Stefan didn't understand. "How?"

Adri guided Stefan's hand to his backside. "Yes?"

Stefan had nodded his agreement before the 'no' he wanted to say reached his lips.

Chapter Five

He could no longer avoid the question he was about to ask, the humiliation. Marije altered her skirts to accommodate her growing belly and his pride grew with it, but neither carried much weight. He had hoped that the sight of another man getting ready to be taken by him would fill him with revulsion, but all he remembered was how much in awe he had been, how moved.

Every new day began with the same thought, ended with the same longing.

Adri had accompanied him home after their usual after-dinner walk. They were standing at the bottom of the stairs. It was still winter and in the dusk the shameful words seemed almost innocent.

"Adri…?"

"You want to ask something?"

"Is there anything you don't want to do with me? Something against your nature?" He needed the reassurance that what he wanted was at least acceptable in his friend's eyes.

"Like what? My whole day is perfect as long as I get to see you for a few minutes. I'm walking on clouds if I get to touch you. You know damn well I'm willing to do almost anything for you."

Stefan closed his eyes and jumped into the dark, deep abyss. "Two men, together, what they do... What we did... Men like you are what you are. I'm a married man and I can't change that either. Nothing can be changed. I've been dreaming the same dream, again and again, since the night Marije became pregnant." His voice became almost soundless. "Do it with me. What I did with you, please do it with me."

He opened his eyes, fearing the dismay on Adri's face, only to see his lover smiling back at him.

* * * *

It was such a luxury to know the landlady was out of town, at the wedding of her eldest niece, and wasn't expected back until after dinner — a whole afternoon without a discreet knock on the door and the question whether the gentlemen cared for a cup of tea! And, in contrast to the few times they'd spent an hour or so in Adri's bedsit room and had fallen into each other's arms like famished dogs on the nearest bite of food, they sat in the moss-green overstuffed chairs and drank coffee. They took their time to make small talk about the weather, smoke a cigarette and to enjoy each other's company as if they had just gotten home from a good day's work.

"Come." Adri stretched out his hand in invitation, and Stefan dropped to his knees next to his lover's chair. He rested his head against Adri's thighs and sighed when he felt the warmth of the muscles through the fabric and the hand playing with his hair. No matter that he had lost almost every certainty about who he was and what he was, he couldn't imagine sharing his body with a man who wasn't at least his equal in strength. Why give his body to a man who wasn't a real man?

His lover caressed his back and whispered, "Redhead."

He lifted his head. "I'm not going to tell a lie and say that my marriage is all pretense, because right up to the moment I met you, I had no idea what was going to happen to me. It's just that now I do know you, I realize I never had any idea what it means to walk next to someone and feel nothing but desperation—because how do I keep my hands to myself?"

"We almost never get the chance to share even a single kiss when we see each other. On those days, I doubt everything and wonder why I had to fall in love with a married man. So often I don't want to meet you, if meeting you comes down to spending the night alone in my own bed, fired up by the knowledge that half an hour's walk away there's you. I hate having to make do with my own hand and always feeling miserable afterward." Adri grinned, so obviously hiding the pain that Stefan felt the hurt in his own stomach. "But today belongs to us. No one will bother us or chase us away. Please, come to bed?"

For a moment he thought about Marije, about the night that had followed the day he first met Adri, when he had pressed her to allow him to have sex with her because he hadn't understood his true needs. Arms around his middle brought him back, forming a trap he didn't want to escape.

"I want you," Adri moaned between kisses.

Stefan sighed audibly. "It looks so much bigger than usual. How's that supposed to fit? I'm not a woman or that kind of man."

"You don't have to prove anything to me. Not that you love me and not that you're a real man. Have a little faith in yourself, okay?"

Stefan got onto his hands and knees. He felt deeply uncomfortable, but persisted in this position until the embarrassment slowly subsided and all that remained was wonder about it all. He still tensed up when Adri's erection brushed the back of his legs, as much worried about the physical pain as fearing it wouldn't hurt at all and what that would imply. The thrill of being in love made it possible for him to surrender with undeniable joy, despite the doubt and the guilt.

He shivered when Adri touched his back.

"You don't like this?" He sat upright and Adri kissed his neck. "Still in doubt?"

Stefan didn't know what to say.

"I've been looking forward to this so much, and now I doubt if I even have the right," Adri told him hesitantly.

Stefan got on all fours once more. "I'm ready for you."

Hard flesh pushed against his opening, pushed and pushed, to no avail.

"You don't want me."

"Please, don't say I don't want you." Again the flesh turned iron. He gritted his teeth, clawed his fingers into the sheet.

Adri withdrew. "My first time did hurt a bit, so perhaps it's something you simply have to go through.

But it wasn't unbearable — more like a short, sharp stab and a burn that lasted almost to the end, but most of it actually felt kind of good." He took Stefan into his arms. "At least we gave it a try. Isn't that what counts the most?"

Stefan sighed. "It's not normal for a guy like me, wanting this. I still don't understand it. I've longed for you for months. It made me mad and it hurt like crazy. Almost every night I lie in bed and my guts hurt from not having you near me. So why does my body refuse you now that it finally has a chance? Why isn't spit enough? It worked well enough for you."

"I think that's the answer. I'm so thoughtless and stupid." Adri stood up from the bed and walked toward the door. "Back in a second."

And sure enough, before he had time to process the information and react, Adri had already returned. Stefan saw him standing there with a cup of salad oil in his hands, his eyes beaming with joy. "That's what we need, something to make it nice and slick. As a carpenter, you probably know that even better than I do."

Stefan held up his hand and Adri poured a little bit of the oil into the palm. He curled his hand around his lover's cock and pumped up and down until the whole surface was slick with oil. Then, once again, he gathered his courage from wherever he could find it. It still hurt, and he recognized the ever-present burn Adri had talked about, but it wasn't so bad — though he didn't quite understand why his lover had talked about pleasure. Something was there, inside him, something foreign and incompatible with the man he was in his own mind.

Adri started to move, slowly and carefully at first, but faster and with increasingly powerful strokes when Stefan didn't protest.

"I'm close. You want me to pull out?"

"No," he heard himself say.

Adri pushed him farther down, keeping Stefan from losing his balance with increasing effort. Finally Stefan had no choice but to follow the fast, aggressive thrusts. His lover seemed to forget him, lost in his own pleasure. He wanted to scream in pain and anger and loneliness. From deep inside a sound welled to the surface that he pushed back because he refused to be that weak. His teeth started to chatter uncontrollably. Then everything was still and motionless and he dropped flat on the bed, Adri's lean-muscled body covering him.

"Are you okay?"

Stefan didn't know what to answer. He had jumped over his own shadow, but the words to describe what it actually meant evaded him. Words like bride and groom, wedding night, had lost all meaning. He smiled and allowed Adri to take him in his arms. The heavy weight of his existence was finally lifted from his mind, if only for a short moment. Adri looked for his tobacco and a minute later they shared a cigarette, smoking in silent contentment.

"Of course I have no real experience except for this afternoon with you, but I doubt many men would be courageous enough to allow this to happen to them." Adri stubbed out the cigarette in the cup with the remaining oil on the night table, turned to Stefan and kissed him. "Thank you for giving me that one chance."

"You don't want to do this again?" Stefan couldn't suppress his disappointment. The unknown landscape has scared him witless, but the idea of never going there again was more frightening than the knowledge that he had stepped over the sacred threshold between his masculinity and something he didn't even dare to name.

"Oh, I do want this again. I want to do so much with you. I just assumed you didn't enjoy it, and I'm happy enough to get on my hands and knees for you whenever you ask me to. Or do something else, like this." Adri dove between Stefan's thighs and licked the shaft of the rested penis with one slow, teasing move. He looked up and grinned. "Shall I go on? I know you haven't come yet and so…"

"You mean that? I wouldn't dare ask my wife to do it. To be honest, the idea never even crossed my mind." Where did the possibilities end? Would they ever reach that point?

Adri took the head of Stefan's cock into his mouth and started to suck gently.

Stefan moaned. "I need… I…"

Adri understood so perfectly what Stefan didn't know to ask for, that Stefan was almost in panic by the time he tapped his lover on the shoulder to warn him he was very close, but Adri ignored him.

"Interesting taste, takes a bit of getting used to but I actually like it." Adri licked his lips for the remaining trace of seed.

Adri covered the both of them with a blanket and in his arms Stefan felt a peculiar sadness. Within the hour they would have wiped out every trace of what had happened between them, like evidence of a crime.

"I want to spend a night with you, so I can watch you sleeping," Adri said.

Stefan ignored him.

They tried to stretch the hour until breaking point, but Stefan was on his way to his wife and children long before the landlady stepped out of the train.

* * * *

He walked home, weak in the legs and light in the head from what had happened that afternoon. He was afraid and confused, and so full of joy he was almost surprised that no one passing turned to look at him. Not wanting to face Marije in this condition, he decided to take a detour. It had happened. He had gone to the room of a man — and the man had taken him like a man takes a woman.

But he wasn't a woman, and he certainly didn't feel like one. So why had it happened to him? Why had he wanted it? He had a wife and he had fathered three children with her, and the fourth was on its way, but for the first time he didn't know what to call himself. He didn't exist. Never had he been this much aware of his flesh and bones and skin, but neither had he ever been this tangled in the maelstrom of his thoughts.

Not until he had walked past the public urinal did he realize that he wouldn't make it comfortably home, so he turned back a few paces and entered. He ignored the sharp smell of the pee of dozens of men like he always did, but he couldn't fool himself that he was able to open the fly of his trousers and pull out his dick with the same thoughtless ease as usual. He was aware of every small gesture, of the difference between his own hand and that of his lover. He was a married man of nearly thirty, and for the first time in over eight years someone other than himself had touched his private parts.

A man entered the urinal and stood next to him. The sound of a zipper going down made him ignore the most important rule, never to look, and he glanced sideways. He didn't just happen to see. He looked, for what must have been seconds. The stranger, who seemed aware of the bold stare, touched himself. Stefan couldn't bring himself to avert his eyes, even though he knew all too well what would happen. Only then the man looked back, touching his semi-erect penis in obvious invitation.

He had been recognized for what he was. His camouflage, that was supposed to make him anonymous, had proved to be useless. The wordless smile, the pumping hand showed how recognizable he actually was to those in the know. As much as he had longed to touch his lover, he had absolutely no desire to stretch out his hand toward this stranger. And yet, for a fraction of a second, he thought that was exactly what he was going to do, and he almost felt the weight of the stranger's erection in his hand.

"You can touch it, if you want to," the man whispered.

It was enough to wake Stefan from his almost hypnotic state. He zipped up his trousers and anger drowned him like a flood. "Men like you make me sick," he hissed, and he pushed the man aside so that he could flee the urinal.

"Coward."

The word was still echoing in his ears when he got out the keys to his home.

Chapter Six

Stefan took every opportunity to see Adri, even if it was only for a few minutes in the stairwell or a short walk through the park. During one of those walks, they discovered that once a week they each rented a book from Huyzen's bookshop and lending library. What could be more logical than to go together on a Saturday, in the afternoon? Even if Marije asked him to allow Sientje to come along, it was still another chance to be together, and Adri assured him he genuinely liked the shy, sweet-mannered seven year old.

That particular Saturday, Stefan had handed in his adventure novel and asked Jakoba Huyzen if she had another book in the same style. Just at the moment when she returned with a title she was sure he hadn't read before—and she was never wrong about that— Adri entered the shop. Stefan didn't do any less or more than what he would have done when meeting any acquaintance. He said hello, made a joke about the weather. Only when he saw the half-inquisitive, half-understanding look in the bookseller's eyes did he realize that Adri and he were grinning in the silly, mindless manner of all people in love.

"I've put aside that Louis Couperus novel you asked about, the one about Heliogabalus," Jakoba said to Adri.

To his surprise, Stefan noticed that Adri seemed to be overcome with shyness for a moment.

"Thank you. I've wanted to read it for quite a while now."

"Perhaps you might enjoy it too, Stefan." Her voice had a friendly tone balanced between the professional courtesy of the shopkeeper and the genuine warmth of friendship. Stefan had known her since the day he had entered the bookshop with a five-cent piece in his hand to borrow his first book. She had been a young woman then, actually a girl. They'd become friends, the way she became friends with so many of her customers, whether they were spending a few cents on one borrowed book a week or buying enough to start a library of their own. She did her best to find any book a reader asked for, and Adri had told Stefan that she ordered books and pamphlets most bookshop owners didn't want to touch. Her thin-as-a-rake, formless body, which no man had ever looked at with passion, contained a large and complex heart.

Whether she actually did suspect that the men—who started to visit her shop together after she had known them separately for years—were lovers, was something Stefan could only guess. The fact remained that she suggested certain titles and Adri gratefully took the books home to read, but she also handed Stefan children's books, as if she wanted to remind him of the life that would always be there. That was why he couldn't understand the reason she told them to search among the rows of bookcases at the back of the shop. She never allowed anyone to take those two small steps down, yet she told them to go ahead. Quickly she pointed out the several categories. "Detectives, romances, general literature, children's books, all alphabetically by writer's name. Take your time while I help a few other customers."

Not sure what to think of Jakoba's behavior, Stefan looked for the book with fairy tales. He had promised Sientje he would borrow it, because she still so much enjoyed being read to by her dad before going to sleep. The moment he took the volume from the shelf, he realized that the bookcases had been placed at such an angle that he and Adri couldn't be seen by anyone standing in the part of the shop where customers waited to be served. He was certain Jakoba didn't know about this, but the idea that he and Adri had a few minutes of what almost felt like privacy made him blush. A broad smile on his friend's face showed he too was aware of their invisibility.

They might have been invisible but they still could be heard, and they made sure to keep their conversation strictly neutral while their hands found each other when reaching for the same book or their lips touched a cheek or an ear. Stefan was embarrassed by the thought that he was allowing another man to touch him, but the shame didn't stop him from looking forward to the next time Adri would stand so close that he could actually feel how much his lover wanted him. The frustration that followed was simply an inevitable part of the game, and there was not much to be done about that without the money to buy even an hour of privacy.

Stefan became convinced Jakoba Huyzen knew what was happening, although she kept her usual slightly distant friendliness. But then, what could she have said that wouldn't be met with a firm denial from both Stefan and Adri? No, it was much better to be grateful for the few minutes of almost innocent touches and smiles, and leave the rest to discreet silence.

* * * *

"How long have I known that I fancy men?"

Adri needed so much time to answer the question that Stefan regretted he had even asked it. What was the use of knowing the why of something that shouldn't exist anyway?

"I don't know. It's never been anything else from the moment I saw the youngest son of the coal deliveryman. He had short blond hair and he wasn't afraid of anything, not even the big nasty dog of that family down the street... Zandstra they were called... Doesn't matter. Little Robbie Bakker must have been the first of at least half a dozen. I had such beautiful dreams, and no one to share them with."

"Until the day you stood in line for the control stamp."

"A bloke in front of me forgot to walk on, and the dream became so real that it woke me up."

"It wasn't my dream."

Adri shook his head in what looked like blunt disbelief. "You must have felt something long before that day."

"It never even occurred to me to look at anyone but girls. I got married to Marije — and happily so." Stefan spoke the words with so much emphasis that he hardly believed them himself.

"And hidden deep inside?" Adri refused to give up.

Stefan regretted he had initiated this talk about the subject, but there was no turning back. Adri deserved that, at least.

"Meeting you was a thunderstorm on a bright day. You may have seen it coming from afar, but I didn't even know there were clouds above my head."

"Would it have made much difference? I knew what I was and I still had no idea of knowing you would happen to me." Adri shrugged. "I waited half my life either for it to go away or to please find someone to share myself with, but I wasn't prepared for you. A bit of fumbling with another boy can't be compared to the moment a man takes you in his arms and everything changes."

Anger rose inside Stefan and he challenged him. "What change? I'm married and I don't see any reason why that wouldn't be possible for you too, in a few years' time. You're as much a man as I am, Adri. You're not like those men…"

Adri shook his head. "You think I'm talking about doing it, the first time you and I did it? No, this is about you, not about you-know-what, as unforgettable as that was for me. You can't be replaced by anyone, man or woman, even though I'm not naïve enough to think there might never be another man sharing my bed during the rest of my life. And the thing you said about me getting married? Please…"

"Why did you fall for me?" Stefan talked quickly past his emotions.

Adri frowned. "How am I supposed to know that? It just happened, the way love always seems to happen for one reason or the other."

"Did you see something in me? I mean, people like that always recognize each other, don't they?" It was impossible for Stefan to hide his concern. Could it be that a total stranger had noticed something that he hadn't been able to see with his own eyes until that very day?

"Like a secret society? Well, I do admit, some of us aren't able to hide it, try as they might. It all comes down to taking the risk and hoping for the best, my dear. There's no way of knowing whether a man will kiss you or beat you up, or simply laugh and walk away. Almost all men are normal, Stefan, I'd learned that much long before I met you. After we both got our control stamp, I almost panicked at the thought that I'd never see you again. I'd recognized my true love, not the man who would necessarily fall in love with me as well." Adri gently touched Stefan's hand. "And you? I think you still don't quite get what is happening."

"Knowing you are that way and thus falling for a man is one thing. Having been married for several years, being a father and one day you stand in line because you're on the dole and suddenly you can't walk on because you have to see the man standing next in line one last time. That's something completely different."

"Being sixteen and knowing you're like that, even if it means realizing you're different from anyone else. No one talks about it openly, but somehow you catch enough gestures and looks to know the doctors want to cure you and the police will take your name down, even if you haven't done anything wrong yet, because the law is such that it's nearly impossible not to break

46

it. Making sure your boss never gets to know, that your landlady has no reason to throw you out of your room. What do you mean, easier?"

Stefan tried to soften his voice as much as possible, as if to compensate for the harshness of the words. "It must be so hard for you to be this unhappy."

Still Adri must have heard the challenge, not the sympathy. "What man in love could ever be unhappy? Who has the right to judge me? Am I a thief? Do I refuse to work for my daily bread? Do I bother people who don't want to associate with me?"

"You're doing it with a married man."

"That married man is doing it with me."

Stefan decided it was better to ignore that remark, and Adri was civil enough not to mention it again. He changed the subject. "Was Marije your first girl?"

"Why are you asking this?" Stefan mistrusted Adri's reasons for such a personal question. "Does it matter if she was my first or my fifth? Would it change anything for you?"

"I want to know the man you are."

"I was visiting great-aunt Neel for her seventieth birthday and I saw the daughter of her next door neighbors. She had a smile to make everything better. I thought she was the nicest person I had ever met." Stefan didn't need to pretend the warmth in his voice, because these were truly fond memories of a growing friendship. "After a year we got engaged, and married as soon as we were able to."

"So Marije was your first," Adri teased.

"I had walked in the park with a girl before or stolen a kiss from the maid servant if I had a job with rich people, but nothing serious, no. I guess I was kind of a late bloomer."

"Then there was me."

"With you I lost the calm certainty that I pretty much knew what to expect from life. Even being on the dole wasn't as hard."

Adri bowed his head. "I'm sorry."

Stefan knew Adri meant what he said, but wouldn't take the obvious course of walking away and never coming back. And was he himself any different in that respect, when the chasm between what he believed he should do and what he actually did seemed too wide to cross? "She deserves better than this."

"Please listen to me. You can tell yourself to do what you believe is the decent thing—in your case, stay with your family and take care of them the best you can, as you promised on your wedding day—but you have no control over the cramp in your belly, the sweat on your hands, the hard-on that pushes against the fly of your trousers."

"I can deny it, pretend it isn't there." Stefan refused to give up the illusion that he still had control over what he did and even what he felt, if he tried hard enough.

"You didn't ignore it." Adri threw in logic, as if logic would be enough to persuade Stefan to let go of his feelings of guilt.

"I can't give you what you deserve."

"I don't need your money, because I can support myself. Even if you hadn't been married to Marije, you still wouldn't be able to give me status or respect in the eyes of others. What I do need from you, you give me as much as you're able to. I would rather have a tiny part of what I want with my whole being than everything of something I don't care for."

They had made the longest detour possible, but now they were standing in front of Stefan's home. "I don't want you upstairs with me, because your presence is unbearable to me," Stefan whispered, and he turned the key to open the door.

Chapter Seven

It was a Sunday afternoon and Marije was taking the children for a visit to *Opoe* Doffer's. Stefan had said, as casually as possible, that he didn't feel like joining them today. Marije was heavily pregnant and this was likely to be one of the last times he felt he could safely let her walk any distance while keeping two boys under the age of six in line, even if Sientje did everything in her power as a seven year old to make life easier for her mother. It was also one of the last times Adri and he would have the chance for some privacy, a rare enough treat as it was anyway.

He watched Adri reading a book, and didn't understand how at ease he felt in the company of someone he had done things with that he hadn't even known he was capable of mere months ago. Adri looked up, smiled at him and continued his reading.

"I can't stop looking at you." Stefan felt like a schoolboy staring at his first crush, and despite being a family man, he was as silly and naïve as he would have been as a twelve year old.

Adri kept on reading, even when Stefan knelt down in front of the chair he was sitting in and opened the fastening of his trousers.

Stefan dug up the already forming erection.

"That's got to be one of the most exciting books you ever read," he muttered before he licked the head for a first taste. It was a gesture born out of a combination of his deeply felt need to be fair in all things concerning his physical love for Adri, and just plain curiosity.

"You have no idea how exciting." Adri grinned mischievously, but he still didn't put his book aside. "Interesting taste?"

Stefan wrapped his lips around the head and sucked for a few seconds before he looked up again. "I could get used to it," he said, and continued to suck.

They ended up on the floor together, with Adri full of impatience undressing Stefan, his eyes wide with delight.

"No one ever looked at me this way." Stefan wasn't even nearly ready to accept the other man's gaze in a matter-of-fact manner. "Maybe it's something women don't like to do, only men."

"What kind of way do you mean?" Adri asked with clearly feigned innocence.

"As if you don't simply accept that I want you, but want me just as much. Marije—I shouldn't even talk about this—she's a sweet woman, but she never does or says anything that even hints that she's really interested in me as a man. Doesn't she have the same needs?" Stefan wondered aloud, but hidden there was another, unspoken question. *Did I marry her for exactly that reason?*

"Perhaps women are like that. How would I know? You're the married man here," Adri said between a rapid series of tiny kisses.

Stefan tried to concentrate on what he wanted to say. "You never have to tell me. I can see it in your eyes. Don't get me wrong, she's always been a good wife to me—"

"But..."

"She allows me, but she doesn't want me—first because she didn't want another baby when we hardly have enough money to feed and clothe the three we already have, and the last couple of months because she's so tired with the pregnancy being so far along." Stefan chuckled. "Who am I fooling? Even during the first months of our marriage, when she definitely wanted to have a baby, she never had that look in her eyes."

"Lust," Adri whispered in his ear, and Stefan thought his body could burst into flames. "I want you, Stefan Doffer, and don't you dare refuse me."

* * * *

Carefully Stefan put his newborn daughter, Ida, into Adri's arms.

"She's a red-haired one, just like her daddy." Adri smiled. "I hadn't expected anything else. Your first three children are the spitting image of their mother, but this one..."

Stefan stepped even closer. "You know when."

Adri kissed the head of the tiny creature and gave the girl back to her father. "You smell of baby."

Stefan walked to the bedroom to return Ida to her crib then looked back at his lover. "And of you."

* * * *

He was lying in bed next to his peacefully sleeping wife. He tried not to toss about, no matter how restless he felt, because she both needed and deserved her rest. It would be a small miracle if one of the children didn't need their mum because of a nightmare, an upcoming cold or a visit to the toilet, and he wanted her to have every minute of sleep possible. She was lucky enough that Ida no longer needed her nightly feeding, but she still required her mama's attention. Despite all his good intentions of getting up for clean nappies and chasing scary monsters away, Marije was often done and finished by the time Stefan realized one of children was crying.

He stared at the strip of moonlight shining through the split between the curtains. Since Ida's birth, now almost three months ago, Adri and he hadn't had a chance to touch each other, except for some nervous fiddling at the bottom of the stairwell. He wanted to get up, get dressed and hurry to his lover through the gray streets of their night-covered town. He couldn't help wondering if Adri was looking at the same moon, having the same thoughts.

It was so easy to imagine his lover's face, with the bright blue eyes and the wide smile. So easy to imagine how Adri would start to loosen the buttons of his shirt, pull down the zipper of his trousers, get out of his outerwear, then his underwear. Wait, he'd forgotten his shoes and socks. Okay, first shoes and socks, then all the rest. But finally he was naked.

Adri's chest hair was a bit lighter than the dark blond hair on his head, but gradually darkened in its journey down until it tapered into almost black pubic hair. He had a well-formed body, but without the all-too-pronounced signs of a life of hard physical labor. His hands were too coarse to be called elegant but they were good hands. Stefan had experienced ample proof of that. He had strong, well-formed legs and feet made to go any distance.

Stefan recalled his lover's genitals, mesmerized by the bold statement of masculinity. A full erection of perfect form and size rose up from a thatch of dark pubic hair. A few drops of seminal fluid glistened on the glans. Adri teasingly pumped a hand up and down the shaft, the other hand wrapped around his scrotum. Then, suddenly, he turned around to show his back. He stood there for a while, his legs slightly spread for balance. Nothing about his back suggested that it too would bend with time. The arse was firm.

Stefan wished he could close the remaining distance keeping him from his lover, stretch out his hand and touch him, but he knew the other would simply vanish into the light of the moon and so he remained motionless on his half of the marital bed. There was nothing left but to watch how Adri turned around once more, brought his left hand to his cock and started to masturbate. With a mixture of frustration and emotion, Stefan saw how his lover almost lost his balance when he came. He ached to catch him in his arms, take him to bed and cover him with warm blankets, kiss him on the forehead and whisper his love.

Chapter Eight

He sat next to Adri on what had become 'their' bench in the park. He wanted to say something, anything, but there was nothing to say really. Adri looked sideways at him, looked ahead again and drummed with his fingers on the painted wood.

With envy Stefan looked at the young couple walking past them, arms firmly linked and heads close together. He almost hated them for their innocence, for the endearing picture they formed. He remembered the months before he married Marije, the indulgent smile from a policeman when he stole a quick kiss from his fiancée, the amused looks when they braved the pouring rain to visit the cinema.

He wanted to take the hand of the man next to him in his own, but the accidental touching of his left leg against Adri's right reminded him that even the most modest longings would never be gratified. People were right. This lust had no basis in anything normal people would ever respect or even tolerate. Yeah, so his heart pounded in his throat every time Adri walked toward him. His hands hurt from not being able to touch him, but on what grounds? It should have stopped months ago, should never have started in the first place, with a wife any man should envy him — but it hadn't stopped.

Abruptly Adri got on his feet. "Walk with me?"

They walked through the overfamiliar paths of the neighborhood park, not knowing where else to go and not wanting to say goodbye, though slowly the jobless with empty hours on their hands, the old men chased out of the house by their ever-busy wives and the mothers with prams and toddlers were already going home. Suddenly they were alone in a quiet corner. Under a tall tree they stopped, and before Stefan realized what was happening, Adri kissed him right on the mouth.

With an aggressive gesture born of fear, Stefan pushed him away. "Idiot."

"I want you and you want me," Adri pleaded.

"Tell me something I don't already know."

"I go mad from not being able to hold you or kiss you. Why do you refuse me?" Adri stretched out his hand and gently caressed Stefan's arm.

Stefan didn't simply allow it to happen, he was actually the one getting a step closer, curling his hand around his lover's neck to angle him in and kiss him.

"We can't do this. It's too dangerous."

They kissed again.

"We have to stop before we get all turned on."

Once more, they kissed.

"Please make it stop." Adri's hands were touching all over. "Please..." He pressed Stefan's body closer against his own. "Please, love, make it stop."

"Then tell me how." Stefan held his friend in his arms, trying in vain to shield him from the pain that was already becoming a fixed element of their love.

Reluctantly Adri retracted from Stefan's embrace. "We'd better go home. Your wife is waiting with dinner."

Stefan nodded in sad agreement. "She's got her hands full already with the baby, and the boys are getting wilder by the day." It took him several seconds before he noticed the tap on his shoulder, and even when he turned around and looked into the face of a policeman, he hardly understood what was happening.

"You don't want to attract any further unwanted attention, so perhaps it's better if you walk with me to the police station." The officer sounded calm, almost friendly, as if he needed to deal with a minor traffic incident. They didn't ask the reasons, didn't try to run away. Stefan felt a slight disbelief, as if he didn't quite understand why they had been arrested. At the same time the intangible fear had become concrete and simply left his body.

* * * *

He barely dared to look at Adri's face, because whatever he thought he would find in his lover's eyes was going to hurt like hell.

He and Adri stood at the bottom of the stairwell of the Doffers' home, each waiting for the other to say something.

"They wanted to know if I was of legal age, or else they could have arrested you for violating Article 248bis of the Criminal Law. Bad luck for them that I'm over twenty-one, so we were only violating public decency." Adri stared at his shoes. "That policeman asked if I was aware of the fact that I was dealing with a married man, if I made a habit of such behavior, and he said I was too young to throw away my whole future as a healthy and apparently normal man. Did I know I could be cured with the help of a psychiatrist?"

Stefan shook in anger. "How could I do this to my wife and children? Didn't I have any feelings of shame? Yes, damn it, I am ashamed, because I can't give my wife her freedom back without throwing her and the children into poverty or making her the object of disgrace, as if they were the ones doing something wrong. It's all my fault."

"You're in trouble?" Adri sounded very concerned.

"Not this time, because of Marije and the new baby. They're willing to forgive me this time and won't press further charges on the condition that I start behaving like a normal man again. They let me go with a warning, but they said I wouldn't be this lucky next time."

"I can't do this to you any longer. I'm a single man. I know what I'm made of and the consequences of what I am, but there's too much at stake for you." Adri looked Stefan right in the eye, then looked down again. "Send me away and I'll promise I'll never bother you again as long as I live."

Stefan understood the significance of the gift but didn't have the illusion he was strong enough to accept it. "If I had any choice, I wish I'd never met you — and even then I would still willingly go and stand in that queue at exactly that moment."

Adri looked up and they both smiled their sad smile. Stefan suddenly realized their shocking visibility, because for the first time their love had left a trail of ink on paper. For the first time their existence had been recognized.

"I have a couple of guilders to spare. There's an address that's pretty reliable. They're not going to ask questions there. What about it?" Adri put his hand on Stefan's arm and Stefan nodded his consent.

* * * *

Adri put the money into the outstretched hand of the woman. Stefan wanted to snatch the coins back from the pocket of her apron and run away. There was too much unsafe distance between this place and the marital bed he called his own.

She looked sharply at them before she ushered them up the stairs, opened the bedroom door and showed them in. "I want you out within the hour. Your kind doesn't need half that time, so I'm not buying any excuses."

The room had nothing about it worth noticing or mentioning. There was a bed, a chair, a small table with a water jug and bowl. It all looked reasonably clean, although Stefan doubted Marije would agree with him on that. She certainly would have told him to whitewash the ceiling, find some cheap wallpaper and what could a bit of paint for the door and skirting boards possibly cost if he asked for leftovers?

"I found this place via an acquaintance. One of us, of course. A good address, I promise you." Adri didn't seem to notice Stefan's doubts, but perhaps it was a good address in comparison with a stairwell or a public urinal. "She can get into serious trouble with the police for this. She must really need the money. Or perhaps she's a tough one, who pretends to have no idea what's going on."

"I can't do this. Can we please leave?" Stefan sat on the bed. There was something undeniably dirty about the room, though he doubted it had anything to do with washing soda and soft soap. The thought of undressing to surrender to his lover's caresses seemed unbearable in this environment.

"I know this isn't the bridal suite of a luxury hotel, but they wouldn't accept us anyway. It's this and not much else, if we want to do it laying down from time to time." Adri knelt down and loosened the laces of Stefan's shoes.

Stefan didn't stop him, accepting the facts for what they were.

Adri told him to lay down and he started to explore Stefan's body as if it were the very first time he had seen Stefan naked. His hands traveled over shoulders, chest, belly, arms and legs like a blind man discovering the reality of a body not his own. He spread his fingers wide to touch as much skin as possible at the same time, kneaded muscles, weighed the scrotum in the palm of his hand, pulled the foreskin down, pressed on the skin between penis and anus, pulled the cheeks apart, pressed a finger inside.

"What are you doing, man?"

"I'm scared as hell I'll forget you," Adri explained, but what was that supposed to mean?

"Forget?"

Adri's hands kept on moving and touching. "Don't think about it, redhead."

"What is it about my hair?"

"You're telling me in all honesty that you don't already know?" Adri looked genuinely surprised.

"Some people laugh at it, some only stare."

"It makes me randy for you." Adri played his fingers through Stefan's chest hair. "Absolutely every hair on your body is a variation of red or ginger or whatever words you use for it, even the hairs on your balls or between your cheeks. I would have fallen for you if you had been blond or brown, but I do love how you look."

Even after a year, Stefan could hardly believe he was able to make another human being this happy simply by existing. The calm contentment of a marriage between two gentle souls who mean nothing but good things to each other, but without unrealistic dreams, the gratitude for healthy children, it had honestly meant something to him.

But then this had happened. Someone had come into his life, someone with lights in his eyes, who touched whatever he was curious about or greedy for, with a body that demanded to be touched back, and suddenly being content to get old and die knowing a good life had been lived was no longer enough.

Marije had been nothing but a good wife, a caring mother and an excellent homemaker. She respected him, even in times when the little money he brought home was handed out to him in return for good behavior and the proper showing of shame and humility. He saw it in the way she prepared his meals, mended his clothes and told everyone how much their youngest looked like her papa. She always tried her best to meet Stefan in his sexual needs, and that was more than he deserved — but it wasn't enough.

A kiss brought him back from his thoughts. "Still upset about what happened?"

"I could have lost everything. And still I'm here, with you, in a room rented out by the hour. I'd rather be here with you than anywhere else. That's the worst of it."

Adri grabbed a tin of Vaseline out of the pocket of his trousers. "I'll show you how happy I am you're here with me."

Hardly more than fifteen minutes later, they were on the streets again, taking great care not to touch each other, even by accident.

* * * *

Extremely limited funds due to irregular employment and — as far as Stefan was concerned — running out of excuses to stay away for hours when he was expected to spend time with his family, were enough reasons to rent the room only on rare occasions. It would never be a place to feel at home, but it had lost the menace of unwelcoming strangeness.

Adri asking, "Do you have time the day after tomorrow?" was enough for Stefan to count the hours, willingly ignoring the still-sane part of his conscience.

Lying in his lover's arms after satisfying their most urgent needs became almost more important than the deed itself. The infrequent moments were precious and he savored every second. Even when he dozed off for a few minutes, Adri continued his touches. Stefan found him once between his thighs, caressing his resting penis.

"Not going to happen. You totally wore me out, lover."

Adri smiled, kissed the very top of the head and stretched his full length alongside Stefan's body. "As soon as I find a regular job, we can rent this room more often." He was all too aware of Stefan's situation, but as he said, "Even when a man has almost nothing, he can still have his dreams. If I had the money, I would buy your freedom. I would go to your wife and say, 'You and the children will never want for anything ever again, but that man is mine'."

Stefan had learned to smile about it. He was wiser now than to state the obvious about the impracticality of his lover's fantasy.

Still rosy from their lovemaking, they opened the front door, only to be stopped by the woman renting them the room. "Don't take it personally, but this was the last time. I don't want to see the two of you at my door again. Have a nice day."

The cold of the falling night made Stefan shiver when he saw his lover walk away.

* * * *

The hawker did a good job with the worthless trinkets he was trying to sell, inasmuch as many stayed a bit longer to watch and listen to his quirky humor. If the merchandise went for cents apiece, his jokes didn't cost even that. Laborers, office workers and shop assistants all sought out the first warm day of spring, keen on anything to break the monotony of the long working hours. Jobless mixed among them, eager for any kind of distraction.

Stefan chuckled. "That man is too good at what he's doing. He's never going to sell anything. Everyone is too distracted to get out their money." He turned to Adri.

"What? It's funny, yes," his friend mumbled absentmindedly.

"Want to walk on?"

"Stay." Adri's voice went to a hoarse whisper.

Stefan froze. He forgot about the hawker, but couldn't forget they were surrounded by dozens of strangers.

Lips brushed his ears. "You're so close I can smell you. Your scent gets me all worked up."

"What...?"

"Give me your hand. Feel me."

Stefan did as he was told, his curiosity marginally greater than his fear, and with the back of his hand, he brushed against Adri's trousers. "Hard."

"My coat is hanging open. No one will notice anything." Adri was so close that their bodies touched. Somehow he had managed to open the fly of his trousers, because he gripped Stefan's hand and led it to the opening.

"God damn it," Stefan cursed, but his hand slid inside and his fingers curled around the erection. It took him hardly more than half a dozen strokes before he retracted his hand, wet with ejaculate. In blind panic he walked away, not stopping until he reached the corner of one of the side streets.

"What the hell got into you?"

Adri at least tried to look guilty, though he succeeded only partially. "I was standing behind you, and the way you smelled reminded me of the last time we did it. I simply couldn't help myself."

"Someone could have seen us and told the police. Have you forgotten we've been arrested once already? I can't afford a second time."

"I'm so sorry. I... This is so... I don't know... I'm only human, Stefan, and I get so frustrated. I need your hands on me. You understand?"

"I can't resist you when you're like that," Stefan admitted. "But please, don't ever do that again."

Chapter Nine

There was no way around it. After more than a year, Stefan couldn't fool himself into thinking it would go away all by itself. Not after all that had happened. The arrest in the park, the fact that they were no longer welcome in the hourly rented room, everything told him that next to none of the normal people he knew would ever approve of the love between two men. Even mere tolerance was evidently too much to ask. And weren't they right about that too?

It had to stop, or not only would his own life be in ruins but that of his family as well. Without much confidence in the result, he visited their family doctor, De Jong. The man wouldn't understand, but at least he was bound by his oath never to reveal to anyone what his patients told him within the four walls of his practice.

"Doffer?" Doctor De Jong was visibly surprised to see him. "What brings you here? Is everything going fine with the youngest? She must be growing like a cabbage.

But, what are the problems? Troubles with the back? A nasty cough?" He was a middle-aged man who had seen babies grown into adult men and women. He had handed out advice, pills and potions against every ailment imaginable, sat at the bed of the dying during their very last moments. Stefan had always accepted the man's authority and knowledge, but this time he couldn't bring himself to say what he had to say.

"Come, come, it can't possibly be anything to scare this old doctor," De Jong encouraged him with a fatherly smile.

"I don't know how to start."

"That is a start. Let me guess. It's about your marriage and you'd rather not talk about it with your wife? Whatever it is, many married men with young families have sat in that same chair across the desk from me."

"I've nothing to complain about, with a wife like Marije and four healthy children. Even work is better now—not perfect, but the very worst seems over." Stefan took a deep breath. Either he must say what he had to say and accept the doctor's advice, or stop feeling sorry for himself. "There is something the matter with me. I don't understand it myself. Perhaps you're not even the one to talk to about it."

"If that is the case, then it's up to me to be the judge of it and refer you to the right expert, wouldn't you think?"

"A bit more than a year ago, I met someone when I was standing in line for a control stamp for dole money. We started to talk and I even introduced him to Marije."

"Yes?"

"Marije quite likes him, and she enjoys it when he visits us for a cup of coffee or a game of cards. He gets along great with the children too."

"You're concerned your wife might commit adultery with your friend? Is jealousy your problem? I know your wife, Doffer, and she's as faithful and honest as any man could wish for in a spouse."

"Marije? What are you insinuating? Of course she would never do something like that."

"Then why this jealousy?"

"Why would I be jealous? It has nothing to do with Marije, at least not in that sense. It's me. I'm the problem in our marriage. Since the moment I met him, I've been having these feelings I never thought possible." Stefan paused. "I've been in love ever since."

Doctor De Jong laughed. "A man of your age, a married man, a family man, should know the difference between friendship and love by now."

"I know the difference," Stefan snarled, then, softer, "Doctor, when you see me like this, what do you think? Please, be honest."

De Jong raised his eyebrows. "What do I see? A healthy, masculine man with a lovely wife and four wonderful children. I see a Dutch working-class family at its best. I've met several of the sexually perverted in my practice, during the nearly forty years I've been a family doctor, and take it from me, there is nothing — and I do mean absolutely nothing — that connects you with those tragic individuals. I admit I'm not a psychiatrist, but I've seen enough to be able to put your mind completely at ease about this."

"I wouldn't want to hurt Marije for anything in the world, but this is making me desperate. I'm getting into trouble and if this continues for much longer, my family will pay the price. They deserve better, and that's why I'm here." Saying the words made him realize how tired he was, and how much he wanted someone with authority to tell him what to do.

"Pull yourself together! You're making a mountain out of a molehill. I doubt much has happened between that man and you. It would be too much against your nature."

Stefan started to mumble. "I can't say what I've done and you don't want to hear it."

"Are you a practicing homosexual?" The doctor demanded an answer.

"You're asking if he and I had intercourse? We did — and just about anything else two men can do together."

"Please, spare me the ugly details. Get a grip on yourself. Crawl into bed with your wife tonight and remind yourself you're a man. Forget about that so-called friend! It was his idea, I presume?" De Jong didn't try to hide his sharp condemnation behind neutral politeness.

"We both wanted it," Stefan defended his friend. "The first time I gave myself to him, I asked for it. He never forced anything on me, ever."

The doctor shook his head, as if he didn't believe he had to hear this from one of the most decent and healthy patients he had seen in his long medical career. "It sounds more serious than I thought at first. Have you tried making it absolutely clear that you don't want his attentions? Is something missing in your marriage? I can understand that you're patient with her, now that she has her hands more than full, and young mothers sometimes forget they are nonetheless responsible for their marital duties. The little one is sleeping through the night by now? I've examined your wife and she's physically healed from childbirth, so it's about time to have regular intercourse with her again."

Stefan couldn't bear to hear the man suggesting that Marije was in any way responsible for his problem. "She never refuses me, except that she asks me to be careful because we can't afford any more children. You know as well as I how much she loves being a mother, but we still have to feed all those little mouths. She is what every normal man wants, but when I'm with her, I dream about him. Day and night he's in my thoughts. Always."

"In all my years as a family doctor, I've seen my fair share of human tragedies, and the drama of the perverse sexual drive is by no means the least of them. A deeply inverted man can only be cured with the greatest effort and the results of treatment are often disappointing. Strict abstinence is the only useful and ethically sane advice one is able to give in such cases. But those who commit themselves to these unsavory acts out of temporary confusion have no reason to give up hope." De Jong paused. He looked at Stefan with stern eyes. "Stop this ridiculous behavior before you destroy a fine and healthy family. The road to recovery is still wide open to you. You'll see that performing vigorous intercourse with your wife a few times a week is the best way to full recovery. In less than a month, you'll be laughing about the whole situation."

Relieved, Stefan left the room, full of hope that he was on his way to being and acting normal again. The truth hurt, but evidently he needed this pain as a reminder that he should dedicate his life to his marriage and his family. This time he was determined to persevere.

* * * *

You won't like what I'm about to say, but please hear me out... Stefan practiced the same words over and over in his head. He prepared for Adri's pale face, the shock in his eyes, the sadness. He mustn't allow himself to be deterred by it. Whatever his body said it wanted, he was going to ignore the stirring in his loins. Adri might be one of those who couldn't help what they were, but surely even he would agree that a man like Stefan had no reason at all to continue with behavior that was simply wrong on all counts. It had to stop before it grew into a craving that would ultimately destroy the good reputation and happiness of a family.

The next day the inevitable happened. He kept a few steps' distance from Adri, who looked at him with eyes that understood what Stefan was about to say but still held a last flicker of hope. The wide, familiar and oh-so-dear smile was frozen on his face.

Stefan put his hands, clenched into fists, in the pockets of his coat. "It has to stop. You and I can't see one another anymore or else I won't know how to resist you. Doctor De Jong is right. I should be with my wife instead of allowing you to fondle me at the bottom of the stairs of my own home." His desperate effort to sound like a man who knew exactly what he wanted would have made him laugh if he hadn't felt so sad and helpless. "You don't have to live like that. Anyway, I hope everything is going to be all right with you."

"All right? Yeah, I'll be all right." Adri shrugged. "You've said what you had to say. I won't bother you any longer."

Sorrow burned Stefan's throat and eyes, prevented him shouting a farewell to the man walking away from him. Friendship had become impossible, too much of a risk if he was serious about his resolution to live as a man was meant to live. Probably he was never going to understand what had motivated him during that year of secret rendezvous and unmentionable filth, and now it was long enough after Ida's birth for Marije to accept his initiative to resume marital relations without question. If she asked why Adri never showed up these days for a cup of coffee and a bit of gossip, he would tell her a white lie about a job in another city.

He would wipe out every trace, until nothing remained that could remind him of Adri Heyman.

* * * *

After his goodbye to Adri, he slept with his wife as often as possible. The dear woman never complained even once, likely because she felt guilty that it had been so many months since the last time. He saw her indulgent smile when she turned on her back several times a week and opened her legs, but not once was there even a trace of desire in her eyes. Her kindness, however, was a balm for his soul, and made his way back toward a fully normal life almost pleasant.

He had found a job. Baby Ida was a happy, healthy girl and her older brothers and sister gave their parents no reasons to complain. When he sat at the table to eat his potatoes, Brussels sprouts and meatballs, Stefan looked at his family and praised himself for having made the right decision.

During intercourse with Marije, hunger for the strong body of a male grabbed him by the neck with razor-sharp fangs, but he ignored it. There was one Sunday afternoon when he was reading a book and he almost sent Marije and the children to *Opoe* Doffer so that he and Adri could be alone for a few hours. There were dreams he never remembered, and he had to force himself not to stare at any man who looked even remotely like Adri.

And every single day, there was this pain in his guts, like a piece of shrapnel from a lost war.

He didn't give in, because he had made his choice as a man and he honored that choice. Doctor de Jong had been right. It was an affliction he could get rid of with the right amount of willpower. It had been much easier than he'd feared. After a month, he was able to tell the doctor he had been cured of the problem.

Chapter Ten

"Is this one as exciting as the last book you recommended me? I couldn't put that one down." Stefan took the Agatha Christie from Jakoba Huyzen's hands, but the sudden sound of footsteps coming from the first floor, where the bookshop owner lived alone, made him almost drop the book. He frowned in annoyance, too familiar with the sound of those footsteps to confuse them with anyone else's, but he didn't want to mistrust his old friend. Adri had never told him he was a houseguest of Jakoba's—but then, why would Adri tell him?

What was going on? Was this some kind of trap? But why would it be? What concern was it of his if two people who shared the same love for books became friends?

"I made him a cup of tea." Jakoba confirmed what Stefan already knew.

"I haven't seen him in a while. Please say hello from me." Stefan could only hope his voice sounded as casual as he meant it to sound.

"You can say it to me in person. I heard you talking." Adri had opened the door between the shop and the private section of the house.

Stefan held up his book and smiled. "Just got another one. You know me, never a day without a good book." He couldn't be weak now. If he showed weakness, what would become of him? He would do what the doctor had told him to do, say a few polite words then leave the other man's company. Friendly but firm, everything would be just fine.

"There's some tea left," Adri said.

This is a test, Stefan realized, but he didn't know the correct answer. Wasn't walking away a sign of weakness? Following Adri to Jakoba's living room and drinking a cup of tea with Adri had its own set of risks. On the other hand, if he managed to drink that tea and go on his way, he would know for certain something had changed for the better and that the whole past year had been nothing but a strange dream.

"I have a few minutes left."

If it was all a trick, at least this was true. The tea was strong and, under the flowered tea cozy, hot enough to burn his lips.

"So, I guess it's all behind you now." Adri certainly didn't beat about the bush.

Stefan nodded. "Would you have wanted to continue like that? Fumbling in dark corners, a stolen hour in a room where, minutes before, a prostitute had entertained her client? Or, if we're very lucky, an afternoon on the bed I share night after night with my wife? That's not a life for a grown man."

"You sound pretty sure of your choice. That doctor has done a good job. If you were me, would you go for help? I'm not married. I've known since forever what I'm made of—but it won't hurt to try, will it?"

"No." The fierceness of his own reaction surprised Stefan.

"Why not? It's working for you."

"You really have to want this, because it's not as easy as it looks. Do you understand?" Stefan accentuated every word.

"What do you mean?"

"I have to avoid all contact with you, pretend there was never any love between us. I have intercourse with my wife as often as possible. And every time I get on top of her, my body feels like that of a stranger. But it's a wonderful success. I don't even want your friendship anymore." Stefan tried to explain the past months.

He didn't want to say it, but he said it anyway. "I'm never without pain."

"If you have that much of an aversion against me, and you're glad we're no longer friends, then why are you here?" Adri's face expressed his anger almost more clearly than his words.

Stefan shook his head vehemently, because he wanted Adri to understand at least this. "That's not how I feel about you."

"Well, you're doing it with your wife and not with me, and you sure sound happy about that. So how am I supposed to understand your words?" The mocking tone in Adri's voice sounded dishonest, but Stefan couldn't blame him.

"I force myself because I want it to work. I couldn't bear it if I bothered Marije two, three times a week for nothing." Stefan finished his tea. This wasn't going as he had expected or hoped. It wasn't Adri's business how difficult it was, how much doubt was eating him alive.

"You made your choice. What do you expect from me? What do you want to hear?"

"Nothing. Respect that I'm a normal guy. A man."

Stefan stood up from his chair and walked to the door, only to stop halfway and return to the table where Adri was still sitting. All his good intentions had crumbled under the pressure of the sudden compulsion to touch the man he still loved. He grabbed his friend's arm, shoved him toward the bedroom and pushed him onto the bed...

They groped and clawed, cooled their aggression on shoelaces and buttons. What was so sacred, so untouchable that they had to pay for it with every ounce of happiness they ever hoped to have?

Stefan trembled with anger when he knelt on all fours and opened his thighs as wide as possible as a sign of surrender. He welcomed the sharp, burning discomfort of being entered too fast, thankful Adri didn't hold back or apologize. He sank his teeth into a pillow and surrendered the totality of his being.

When finally the sharp edge of the pain had been lessened by the violence of their moves, he was ready to take Adri into his arms. "The doctor honestly thought I could get rid of you, like a drunk gets rid of his liquor. He thinks it's always about lust between men, never love."

"Don't I make you horny?" Adri teased and he took Stefan's erection in his hand. He knelt between his legs, bowed low, took the head in his mouth and started a slow, gentle suck.

Sorrow engulfed Stefan with such force that he didn't know where to look for safety. He cried, sobbing and heaving and finally with silent tears. Adri stayed with him, holding him down onto the bed, anchoring him and pleasuring him with his mouth until he had reached his climax, and finally kissing the tears away.

"No one forced me to visit our family doctor and tell him how I feel about you. I wanted to be normal, to be the man I was before I met you. I bothered the woman who didn't desire me and pushed away the man who wanted me more than anything. I've done everything to get you out of my mind and my body. I'm not a good person, Adri. I don't deserve you."

"You're punishing yourself. Please, don't do that." Adri kissed Stefan's forehead and held him in his arms while he continued to talk. "I've seen you drool with lust. I smelled your scent, felt the heat of your skin, seen you come. I know what that doctor will always be blind to. He knows nothing."

Reassured for the moment that he was forgiven, Stefan allowed himself to close his eyes. He was surrounded by his lover's arms. He was safe.

"We have to get up. There's only so much time a man needs to drink a cup of tea," Adri warned him.

"I think Jakoba knows. Perhaps she doesn't know what she knows, but she knows. Surrounded by all those books, she must have learned something." Enjoying the all-too-fleeting moment, Stefan stretched his body, rolled over and kissed his lover as if they had all the time in the world.

"I'm serious. We have to go down." Adri tried to wriggle away.

"You don't want to make up for lost time? Don't worry. Later today I'll worry about us, but please, let's enjoy these few minutes?" Stefan reluctantly made room so that Adri could get up. "You're absolutely sure you're not mad at me?"

"You're absolutely sure you're not mad at yourself for going to the family doctor? Or for being here with me?"

"I don't know. I'm not in a fit state to think about what I feel." Stefan got on his feet, looking for clothes he didn't want to put on just yet.

"It's not like I can refuse you anything..." Adri said indulgently and he lowered his trousers once more and leaned over the bed.

Stefan hesitated for a moment. Should he take this last step? This time he couldn't pretend it was actually someone else making him do this. He was the one who wetted his erection with spit. He was the one who used a finger to open up the man he was about to take. He was the one who placed the head of his erection against the opening and pushed in. He was the one who did all of it—he, and no one else.

* * * *

The weeks that followed his reconciliation with Adri were the happiest in a long time. He remembered how to whistle, how to play street football with his sons, and he even bought a box of chocolates for Marije. No way was he going back to Doctor De Jong to admit his relapse. He saw his lover almost daily and every touch, every kiss was worth the full value of his soul.

But he couldn't ignore the surprised, uncomprehending look in Marije's eyes. How was she supposed to understand when he went from asking for intercourse several times a week, to leaving her alone from one moment to the next? To avoid any questions, knowing all too well it was the only way to keep up the pretense of a normal marriage, Stefan turned toward his wife and stretched out his hand.

She shook her head.

"Wrong time?"

"Not before next week."

"It's been a while, don't you think?"

"Do you want it, or do you think you have to want it?"

The casually spoken question made Stefan retract his hand and prevented him from asking what exactly she meant. He feared her answer enough to try to avoid it at any cost. And she seemed happy enough to kiss his cheek, wish him good night, turn on her side away from him and go to sleep.

What was—and perhaps even more, what wasn't—said was still running through his head when he saw Adri the next day. He didn't long for his wife's body and hadn't done so for a long time, yet her outright refusal shocked him more than he had expected.

* * * *

"It's none of my business, so feel free to tell me to shut up, but how married are you and Marije actually? I mean, you're still having sex with her?"

Stefan looked at him. "Are you reading my mind?"

"I was just wondering, and perhaps I can't help wanting at least that part of you for myself."

"Last night I gave it a try, though I'm not sure why. Because we're married, I assume. It's what I'm supposed to do. She asked me if I wanted it or just thought I should want it."

Adri chuckled. "Ouch."

"I think she has some kind of suspicion something's not right, but she didn't say a word about it."

"Even if she knew, and I really doubt that, what is she supposed to say? I'll take care of myself and my four children if you no longer want me?" Adri stopped at the bench in the park and sat down.

Stefan hesitated, but joined him. "She could tell me to end this."

Adri took his time to roll a cigarette, light it and give it to Stefan. "She's a woman and I know she's a clever one too. I bet she feels there is something going on, having female instincts and all—but that her husband has fallen in love with another man? That he sleeps with him? You really think she'd even be able to come up with the idea?"

Stefan returned the cigarette for Adri to take a pull. "But I know."

"If you send me away again, will that save your marriage?"

Stefan didn't answer that one.

"What are you withholding from her that you were giving her before you met me? Do you give her less household money because you're spending it all on me? Are you neglecting the maintenance jobs around the house? Have you stopped being a father to your children?"

"I take extra care with everything so she doesn't have to suffer as a result of...this." Stefan took another long draw from his cigarette.

"And so last night you came up with the idea that you should have another try at normal intercourse. Did she ask for sex? Did she look at you or touch you in a way that made you think she was in the mood?"

"Not like you." Stefan shook his head. "Not at all, to be honest."

"And yesterday she refused."

"I'm not even relieved." He noticed that Adri didn't understand him, and he didn't expect him to — the same way he didn't expect Marije to understand what had made him fall in love with another man, if she could see at all what was happening right there in her own home. If he were honest, then he had to admit he had become a stranger to himself.

Chapter Eleven

Stefan preferred to stay out of certain parts of Adri's life. Some of Adri's friends were too outlandish to his taste. He wanted nothing to do with the circle of highly educated men, often painters, actors and writers, that tolerated Adri in their midst merely because Jo Swart considered him the son he'd never had. It was at Jo Swart's house that they nearly always met. He was master behind his own front door, and money did the rest.

"What makes you go there? You have nothing in common with them — almost nothing," he asked, not even sure why.

"We talk about books and art, we gossip a bit about who's together and who just split up and someone is teaching me to play chess. I can teach you, if you want." Adri looked at Stefan. "It's somewhere you can be yourself without being judged."

"You told them about us?" Stefan wasn't able to hide his concern.

"What do you think? If I can't shout from the roofs that I'm in love with this wonderful man, at least I can say it to friends who are happy for me instead of telling me I'll go to hell or I'm sick or a criminal." Adri clearly didn't see Stefan's increasing unease.

Stefan couldn't suppress his growing anger. "Are you out of your mind?"

"What's upsetting you? Everything said or done stays within those walls, because every single one of us relies on the discretion of the others. Some still live with their mothers, who aren't supposed to know. Some fear for the loss of clients or employers. Some have high positions at universities or in politics. Some are married themselves."

Stefan still didn't understand. "Actors, writers, university professors, other high-up folks... What do they see in you, a house painter?"

"You think I'm not good enough for them? That I can't talk about books or politics? That I don't have an opinion because I didn't go to school after my fourteenth birthday?"

"I'm sorry. Any man should be proud to call you his friend."

"Now and again someone brings a working-class boy to our meetings. They're all of age, of course. The host makes really sure of that, because it can get a man into deep trouble if he even kisses someone under the age of twenty-one. Without an introduction and the word of someone we all trust, nothing happens."

"Am I not your only one?"

"What...?"

"You heard me." It was impossible for Stefan to back down now.

"On the day I became of age, you were my first and there hasn't been a second one, though God knows my left hand and I grew to be very close friends at times."

"Those people have so much more to offer than I do. I only read simple detective and adventure novels. I know nothing about art or politics. You always have to share me with my family — and they get almost all of me."

Adri touched Stefan's hand long enough for it to be felt but little enough to avoid panic. "You're jealous and you know damn well there's no reason for that."

Stefan didn't dare look into his lover's eyes, knowing all too well how ridiculous his behavior was. "You're a handsome man, so please don't tell me none of them ever tried anything. And wouldn't you prefer a nice educated man you can have all to yourself?"

"Yeah, I can really see that happening — a lawyer or a surgeon introducing me to his family. I'll always be someone's dirty secret, Stefan, with or without money," Adri sneered, though his voice softened right away. "It doesn't matter how different we are. When we're in Jo's salon we're friends first and last, and they know there's only one for me. They care about me because they understand. Someone told me during dinner once about an old acquaintance, a civil servant, who had lost his friend of more than twenty years because of a sudden illness. The family told him in no uncertain terms that he wasn't welcome at the funeral. People like us will never get a fair chance to show we can be just as decent and faithful as anybody else. No one cares how our marriages might look."

"Marriages? Now you really are talking nonsense." Stefan shook his head and burst out laughing.

"Okay, that's a bit too silly." Adri grinned. "But you understand what I'm trying to say? If it's nearly impossible to meet a potential friend in a normal way, if hardly anyone wants to rent houses to couples like us, if we're only acceptable when we make ourselves invisible, and even then…how are we supposed to find out what love means to us?"

"That's not so hard to imagine, is it? We go to work every morning. We have supper, talk about the weather. We play cards and listen to the radio play on Saturday evening. We keep our house neat and clean and… Oh God…" Stefan crumbled.

"In our case you would still be married. It doesn't matter whether I'm a man or a woman because you're too much of a man to leave your wife and family behind in poverty and shame. But do you really think we'd have a fair chance if you hadn't been married? Freedom is for those with enough money not to have to depend on a twenty guilders a week job, for artists and bohemians and perhaps for those who have nothing left to lose anyway. The law is there to protect the normal people from us, but who protects us from them?"

"We manage, don't we? We see each other every day. You're practically part of my family." Stefan knew all too well how unconvincing his words sounded.

"How many times did you try to break up with me? How many times have you said you hate it that you love me? I want a place to feel safe and accepted, to be with you where no one blinks an eye. Is that so much to ask?" Adri sounded so sad that Stefan couldn't stop himself touching Adri's hand, knowing it was at the same time too much and not nearly enough.

* * * *

"Come on, Stefan. It's not like I'm asking you to accompany me to my friends, but please, you have to meet Jo. Without him I would have been lost as a young boy, easy prey for any man who didn't care about the law or my obvious lack of experience. He's a true gentleman, one of a kind," Adri insisted.

"You sound like you want your father to meet your fiancé." Stefan was not entirely sure he was joking, but Adri nodded and said, "I've already told him so much about you, but that's just words. I want him to see that the real you is even better than I could possibly tell him. I've waited all this time for you because he told me it would be worth my patience. Join me tomorrow afternoon?"

Despite his growing list of objections, Stefan visited the neighborhood bathhouse and made sure his clothes were clean and tidy. By now finding an excuse to spend several hours out of the house on a Sunday afternoon, by tradition a time that would ordinarily be used to visit family with his wife and children, had become frightfully easy.

He recognized the avenue where Johannes Swart lived from work—a place with nothing but big, stately homes owned by families who had been rich enough for long enough to have lost all memory of ever having to do a manual job to get by.

"You never told me your friend had that kind of money."

"Why should I have? He helped me to find my way in life, recommended me for a room, work, paid for evening classes but most of all he helped me to become an independent adult. And that can't be bought with money. I have no idea about his fortune, but it must be huge since he hasn't worked for his living for a single day in his life. Can you imagine that, trading in art just for fun? I bet it's made him even richer than he already was. He could afford to be a patron for young artists and poets. He wouldn't miss the couple of hundreds a year anyway." There wasn't even a hint of jealousy in Adri's voice, not even when he said, "With his money, I could settle your family in a nice little cottage close to my own villa, make sure your kids went to proper schools and your wife never wanted for anything, and have you almost entirely to myself."

"You were saying something about being an independent adult? Doesn't that count for me too?" teased Stefan.

"Then we do it the other way around, with you being filthy rich, living in the big house with your family and me in the servants' house. You can visit me any time you like."

"And any time just happens to be every night?"

"Something like that."

* * * *

Half an hour in the company of Johannes Swart— "Please, call me Jo. I insist" —and Stefan understood why Adri spoke so highly of him. The tall, slender man was a true gentleman in every meaning of the word — friendly and courteous without the condescending tone Stefan had noticed almost invariably when he had a job in one of the big houses. He usually wasn't welcome at the front door and always had someone watching him while he was doing his job, as if he was likely to steal something, asking all sorts of personal questions about his family while he wasn't supposed to ask the same questions back. It had made him feel almost as small as when he'd needed to ask for unemployment benefit in order to keep his family alive and with a roof over their head. Not so Jo Swart, who served high-quality coffee in fragile china cups. The chocolate cake that went with it... It was chocolate cake. Who had money for cake these days, let alone one that richly layered with chocolate and cream?

"Can I ask for your opinion on this piece? It's from the eighteenth century, French." Jo pointed at the most beautiful piece of furniture Stefan had ever laid eyes on, a small cabinet of deep dark wood, simple but perfectly balanced.

"You know who made this?"

"Sadly I don't, but he must have been a master in his craft."

"You can see how everything fits together. How..." Stefan suddenly stopped. "I bet you know much more about antique furniture than I do."

"Perhaps, but you actually work with the material." Jo smiled. "Just like I have my philosophies about love and you know its reality."

"I'm not so sure about that."

Adri raised an eyebrow. "He's got the perfect family with the sweetest wife on earth and four healthy children, and you know how I feel about him. The first time I met Stefan and he asked me for a cup of coffee at his place and I saw his wife and the two boys, I knew I didn't stand a chance."

"I was the one who didn't stand a chance." Stefan had to say it.

Jo nodded. "Love knows a way of finding you, no matter how cleverly you think you're hiding. But sometimes you wish..." He didn't finish his sentence.

Stefan sighed.
Adri sighed too.

* * * *

Adri flopped down on what had become 'his' chair, with a face that looked like seven days of extremely bad weather. He didn't say a word, obviously waiting for Stefan to start asking questions.

"Now, tell me what's going on." Stefan placed a cup of coffee and a cigarette before his friend's nose.

"I was at Jo's, me and a couple of other friends. Then someone, a French language teacher of almost forty, no wife or children, told me he had tried to get an advertisement placed in a national newspaper in which he was asking for a male traveling companion. Everything squeaky clean, not one wrong word in the whole text. I've read it myself. And what do you think?" Adri waited for good effect.

"Sounds innocent enough. You can't ask a woman to join you for a vacation, people will start talking." Stefan didn't understand what Adri wanted to say, why he was so angry.

"It was refused, without a reason given. But my acquaintance wasn't born yesterday, and neither am I."

"Perhaps the newspaper folks aren't as stupid as you think. That man wasn't looking for a travel companion, was he?" Stefan suddenly realized. "Travel to where on a teacher's salary, Friesland and back?"

"As if that matters. The text was clean as a whistle and what my friend and any man writing back would want to do is their own business, even if they weren't planning to leave the neighborhood—or even the house. It's their business, no one else's." Adri raised his voice.

"Keep it down, will you? Marije and the kids are at *Opoe's* but I still have neighbors," Stefan reacted sharply. "Isn't it the duty of that paper to protect men who might innocently believe someone was actually looking for company to travel abroad?"

"You clearly have no idea how many men know very well what is actually meant when they read about traveling companions. A grown man doesn't need protection from a couple of busybodies. Do *you* need protection?" Adri challenged.

Stefan hesitated. "To be honest, I don't know. If you say the ad was decent, I believe you, but that paper had to keep to the rules or else they'd be in trouble. A paper or magazine placing just about anything... Can you imagine what would happen? Respectable bachelor of twenty-eight, civil servant, unattached, seeks likewise for special friendship."

"If only... But no, we're not going to see that in our lifetime." Adri took a sip of his coffee. "We can be grateful if we even get a personal ad about travel companionship accepted or for someone who likes to visit the theater. As if it's the easiest thing in the world, finding someone who is also that way. Some of us can't hide that they're different, no matter how hard they try, and they get ridiculed for that. But the rest of us? How do we recognize a like-minded soul if letting anyone know can mean the loss of family or a job? And when we finally go mad for the touch of a man and visit the public toilet, we get arrested for public indecency. So tell me, how are we supposed to meet someone to be a bit less lonely with?"

"We did." Stefan stood up, took the two steps needed to get at Adri's chair and kissed his lover's hair.

Adri leaned into the touch. "We're the exception to the rule, the proof that miracles do happen. Why don't normal people give us a chance for a bit of happiness? Would it hurt if a group of men or women, all over the age of twenty-one, got together a few times a year for a dance and a dinner? How could public decency possibly suffer from a magazine that's only being sent in a plain envelope to those who can prove they are of age?"

"Because it might give young, healthy, impressionable people the wrong idea?"

"You're talking nonsense, and you know it."

Stefan kissed his lover's neck.

"You'd almost think being that way is so wildly attractive to normal men that everything needs to be done to keep them away from it, even if it means unhappy marriages — and as a consequence, miserable individuals. And let's not forget about the risk of blackmail, when that good-looking man who swears he's in his twenties turns out to be nineteen."

Stefan kept on kissing his lover.

"And to think there isn't a day when I don't realize how lucky I am to have met you and Jo and a few others. I met the right people at the right time, but I'm the exception."

"Come to bed..."

Really, what more was there to say?

* * * *

Adri put the board and pieces on the table. "I promised to teach you how to play chess and Jo Swart gave me one of his old sets, so that's what I'm going to do." He must have noticed Sientje's shy but curious looks because he asked her, "You want to give it a try too?"

"Mum? Can I?"

Marije smiled at her eldest daughter. "Go ahead, but don't forget to finish your knitting before tomorrow night or you won't get that ten-cent piece."

To Stefan's slight embarrassment the child, not even ten years old, proved able to pick up the game with relative ease while he struggled to remember the basic moves. It was good, though, to see how much Adri had become a part of his family, and he didn't miss Marije's happy face when she saw her eldest girl being ever so proud to have beaten her daddy in a game of chess.

For weeks many hours after supper were spent perfecting the game, although Stefan decided that watching Sientje and Adri play was actually a lot more amusing than being humiliated by his much-too-cheerful best friend and his daughter. So, when they had a Sunday afternoon for themselves again and Adri asked him for a game of chess, Stefan distracted him by suggesting to his lover that they go to the bedroom and have some fun there instead.

"That way you'll never learn to play on any decent level," Adri mumbled, after a little more than an hour of slow and gentle lovemaking.

Stefan lazily kissed him. "I don't care. Did Jo teach you how to play chess? I'm just curious." He stretched and looked for his clothes. "Sorry, love, but I've got no idea when Marije gets home and…" He kissed Adri to apologize.

"No problem." Obediently Adri dressed and followed Stefan to the living room. He rolled a cigarette and shared it with Stefan. "Jo didn't teach me how to play chess, if you still want to know, but someone we call the Baroness when we're among friends. The man has a brilliant mind, a razor-sharp memory and more feeling for drama than a Hollywood starlet. He's married — and yes, his wife is definitely the one wearing the trousers in that marriage."

"Never in my life had I thought I could tolerate the touch of another man, let alone that I would actually want it, but there are things I'll never get used to," Stefan started, not sure how to say what he wanted to say without offending his friend.

"Like what? If you didn't like anything we did, you sure knew how to hide it. And you only have to tell me and whatever we're doing stops right away."

Adri looked puzzled. "You didn't enjoy what we did in bed?"

"Of course I did, I loved every second of it," Stefan hastened to say. "I'm still ashamed of what I am by having sex with you, but nothing we ever do is against my will. I want you. No, I meant to say that the kind of men you sometimes see on the street makes my skin crawl, though perhaps calling them men is too much of an honor for those creatures. The way they dress and walk and smell... Are they even trying? A man should be a man and a woman a woman." He spat out the words as if trying to get rid of a morsel of spoiled food.

"What are you going on about? This is about the Baroness, isn't it? Or perhaps I should say that it's about you being afraid that by making love with a man you might change into less of a man yourself."

"How can you even stand to be in the same room with such people?"

"They're my friends—not just the Baroness, but also the illustrator of the fairy tales you read to your children and the dancer who performed for Queen Wilhelmina and Princess Juliana. Why wouldn't I feel comfortable in their company? You don't have the right to judge others like that."

"Admit that you're doing it with me because I'm one hundred percent masculine." Stefan refused to give up, though he no longer remembered why. What did he care about people he would never meet anyway?

"So what? That's a matter of taste. Believe me, the men you're talking about as if they're less than dirt have their romances too. I know the difference between sexual attraction and friendship. I don't have to prove how really manly I am by saying how much I hate sissies." Adri's voice betrayed his suppressed irritation.

"Do they even realize how normal people stare at them and talk about them?" Stefan had no idea what was the matter with him. He only knew he couldn't stop himself.

Adri now looked downright angry. "No, they do it all on purpose, because they enjoy being ridiculed and spat at and gossiped about. You don't know how much some of them try to hide, to become normal-looking, and it never works. I'm sorry, Stefan, but I'm not going to refuse people my friendship because of something they can't help and that hurts them more than anyone else. Are you going to dye your red hair into a more acceptable color? And, just so you don't get the wrong impression, if you did that, I'd refuse to have sex with you until your natural color grew back."

Stefan couldn't help laughing. "You look like an angry schoolboy. If I'm really honest, I have to admit I don't care about those men one way or the other. I'm a married man who happens to have fallen for another man. You're an adult, and I can't decide for you whom you consider your friends. Kiss and make up before Marije and the kids get home?" Without waiting for the answer, he pressed his lips on Adri's, teasing with his tongue until his lover granted him access.

Chapter Twelve

They were in such luck that the Sunday they planned on going to the beach was one of the sunniest of the summer of 1938. It had taken Adri some trouble to convince the Doffer family to accept the train tickets, but he argued that all those cups of coffee and meals must have cost them a lot more, and what about simply allowing him this small gesture of friendship? Packages of sandwiches in greaseproof paper, a Thermos with cold tea, a bottle with orange soft drink and as a special surprise for the children, a bag with currant buns and sponge cakes all went into one big basket. Marije filled a bag with swimming trunks, bathing costumes, towels and whatever else three adults and four children might need for a day at the beach.

It was all one big happy adventure for the children, who hadn't seen much of the world except for their own neighborhood, visits to family who lived elsewhere in town and a stay with their mum and dad at their maternal grandparents' home. The walk from the train station to the beach would be too much for Ida, so Adri took the little girl on his neck and carried her all the way. Ida giggled with pleasure. They were the best of friends, the dark blond man and the red-haired toddler.

Marije spread out some of the towels and helped the children change into their swimwear. Stefan noticed her visible pride when she saw that the home-knitted costumes looked just as nice as anything bought in a shop. *Opoe* Doffer had bought them some toys, so the boys could make a sandcastle and Sientje could sieve through the sand to look for shells.

Stefan watched the children play while he ate his first sandwich and drank a cup of cold sweet tea. They were healthy and happy children, obviously being raised by a loving, caring mother and a father who did everything in his power to provide for them. But there were also the pale skins, and the wide-eyed wonder about how big the sea was, shining a bright light on the fact that their little troupe hadn't been spoiled with too many day trips.

Marije smiled at him in acknowledgment, but kept one eye on Ida. She was going to watch her young like a hawk, even when Stefan promised her with his hand on his heart that she could rest for an hour because he would make sure nothing happened with Ida and Wilfred, whose sense of adventure was bigger than his six-year-old self could handle. She visibly enjoyed the sun and the sound of the waves, but if it wasn't for the children, why would she sit on a towel on the beach doing practically nothing?

"You care for a walk?" Adri stood up and stretched his body to its full length. He had told Stefan he had spent a few hours on the flat roof of a friend, and his skin had taken on a slight tan. He was young, in the prime of his life, and Stefan couldn't keep his eyes off his lover, although he hardly dared look in his direction, afraid his woolen swimming trunks would be a dead give-away. "What about getting our feet wet? And does Ida want to join Papa and Uncle Adri?"

The little girl grabbed her unofficial uncle's hand as soon as she heard the words. "Papa?"

Stefan took her other grubby, tiny paw in his own and she skipped through the rippling water without any signs of fear. Selle showed his younger brother his bravery in the cold waves, and so Wilfred couldn't stay far behind. Sientje had her doubts, but finally gave in to the big adventure. Marije watched and waved and shouted, "Not too far…"

Four perfect children with a perfect mother, a perfect lover on a perfect day. Stefan stopped walking and allowed his daughter's hand to slip away. Adri was still holding her hand when he looked over his shoulder and smiled. Stefan's heart blossomed with joy. He joined them again.

"Go to Mama, sweetheart. I think she has a surprise for you." He pointed at Marije, who was waving the bag with currant buns and sponge cakes. Its siren call was too much for the ever-hungry toddler and she ran after her much faster brothers.

"I saw you together, little Ida and you, and I thought, this is your child too. Without you, I wouldn't have made her that night."

"One look and everyone knows she's your child." Adri gave him his special smile. "You think there's a bun left for the grown-ups as well? And after that, I guess it's time to build the sandcastle to end all sandcastles."

* * * *

Later that afternoon they went home exhausted and sunburned. Adri carried the already sleeping youngest child up the stairs, while even the boys were done making noise. For weeks they would show their collection of sea shells to their envious friends, show off about the height of their sandcastle and how brave they had been in the cold and deep water with waves as high as their dad.

"I'll let you out," Stefan said to Adri, who thought it was really time to go back to his own place. At the bottom of the stairs, he took Adri into his arms. "You smell like the sea and the wind. Thank you for today."

"Thank you for saying yes." Adri gently kissed the salt from his lips.

Stefan answered the kiss. "You were so happy and at ease with the children on the beach, and they love you so much and all I could think…"

"What a beautiful man, who helps his sons finding shells, keeps on eye on the toddler while she plays with the waves, holds the hand of his eldest when she's afraid to admit she's afraid of all that water. I want that man in my arms. Those were my thoughts."

"So you and I were thinking the same thing."

"I want to lick the salt from your body and make love with you until the first light of morning. I really don't want to use my hand to bring you off in a hurry or ask you to do the same for me. It would be the wrong end to a perfect day." Adri kissed him one more time and let go.

"I was afraid you would go home with a nasty feeling if I…" Stefan brushed his hand against Adri's crotch.

"Today is all or nothing, and since all is impossible right now…"

He opened the door, watched Adri turn the corner, then closed the door again and went up the stairs to his wife.

* * * *

Adri had stayed for supper that night because Marije had cooked turnip stew with gravy from Sunday's dinner, with semolina porridge sweetened with treacle for dessert, and usually he enjoyed such a meal with relish. This time, however, even fussy eater Selle finished his plate faster.

With a worried look, Marije put the leftovers away. "You don't like turnips? I thought…"

"My own mother couldn't have cooked a better stew."

There was something wrong—Stefan was certain of it—but he couldn't quite put his finger on it. It was all in the details. Not only in Adri's lack of appetite, but also in how he didn't react to Selle's schoolyard braveries and Wilfred's 'I did something very brave too', or had to disappoint Sientje because he really wasn't in the mood for a game of chess. Ida was much too quiet on his lap, as if she too knew her Uncle Adri wasn't himself.

"Care for a walk around the block?" Stefan tried.

Adri shrugged.

Why not ask him? The question was simple enough, and if the answer wasn't meant for the others to be heard, Adri could easily think of some excuse and tell the truth later. Asking, however, might disturb the fragile balance, the calm contentment of knowing life wasn't as bad as he was aware it could be.

After Marije had put the children to bed, Adri was still sitting on his chair, pale and quiet, staring at the coffee he had allowed to become lukewarm then cold.

It was obvious to Stefan that his friend wasn't at ease for some reason, but why didn't he simply get up and go home to get a good night of sleep and whatever it was? It was bound to be only half as bad in the morning.

"How's your new boss? And the other blokes? You get along well?" Marije tried.

"Yeah, they're okay."

Another silence that lasted for seconds but felt like minutes.

Why didn't he look at Stefan to flirt with him while Marije washed the coffee cups in the tiny kitchen? Why didn't he stretch out his hand over the table, and Stefan could do the same until their fingertips touched for a split second and both would grin and say, "Sorry."

Just before Stefan had had enough of it and wanted to suggest his friend come back when he was in a better mood, Adri stood up slowly. "Thanks for supper. I'm going." He took a step toward the door, hesitated and looked helplessly at Stefan. "I..."

Stefan had never in his life moved as fast as he did right then, and still he was barely in time to catch Adri in his arms and prevent his head from smashing against the sharp corner of the table. Marije was only a second behind. Together they put him back on his chair.

"What just happened? Did you hurt yourself?"

Adri dizzily shook his head, confusion in his eyes.

"There's something wrong with you, isn't there?"

Stefan didn't even try to hide his concern. He looked at his wife. "Marije…?"

Marije studied Adri's face for a moment, then she made up her mind. "We can't let him go down the stairs in this condition. It's simple. Tonight he sleeps in our bed, because that's the only decent place for a sick man. We'll find a solution for ourselves in a minute, but first he needs our help." With the experience of many childhood illnesses and bouts of fever in her hands, she touched Adri's forehead. "Poor guy, the fever is burning him up. How is it possible we didn't notice anything, except that he was awfully quiet and hadn't much of an appetite?"

"Shall we put him on the bed? I don't think he can sit upright much longer," Stefan suggested and together with his wife, he helped their friend onto the bed.

"What do we do now?" Stefan asked. "You know about these things, when it's necessary to call for a doctor and such." It was her decision — always had been, always would be.

Marije looked closely at the man lying on the bed, touched his head once more. "If it doesn't change overnight, we might need a doctor, but I trust it for now. We'll keep a close eye on him in case he suddenly gets worse."

"What's wrong with him all of a sudden? We had a nice long walk yesterday after work and he was perfectly healthy then." He was too worried about Adri to wonder if Marije heard and understood the tone in his voice. And, even if she had, it wouldn't matter because she understood what it meant to care for people.

"It can happen from one moment to the next. A person gets an infection and within a few hours, he's got a fever so high the thermometer can't measure it." She looked genuinely concerned. "Let's hope for the best. Help me get his outer clothing off. That'll be much more comfortable for him. I'll get a pair of your pajamas. They should more or less fit."

When Adri was lying as comfortably as possible between the sheets, they went back to the front room, keeping the sliding door open enough to see and hear if Adri needed them. Marije made some hot milk with aniseed and they drank slowly.

"And where do we sleep? I'm getting tired and I bet you could do with some sleep too." Stefan yawned.

"We can put up a makeshift bed here in the room. We still have that old stretcher in the attic. Could you get it for me?"

Stefan nodded.

"Please be quiet so the boys don't wake up. "

Hardly more than ten minutes later, Marije had made the bed.

"The two of us will never fit on this thing. It looks like it's on its last legs anyway. Give me a couple of blankets and I'll sleep on the floor. I've had worse when I did military service."

Marije shook her head. "There's no need for you to do that."

"If you think I'll allow my wife to sleep on a couple of blankets on the cold, hard floor you're very much mistaken." Stefan threw in his formal authority as a final argument.

"What are you going on about? In the room right next to this there's a perfectly fine bed and I know for certain two people fit easily. There's only one person in that bed right now," Marije started.

"What?" Stefan couldn't believe what she was saying.

"You think I'm going to climb into bed with a man I'm not married to? Really, Stefan, sometimes I think… No, you sleep in your own bed, and I sleep here. That's easier for the children too, in case they need me." Marije shook her head. "Men…"

"A man isn't supposed to share a bed with another man."

"Says who? You're the best of friends and you've got to sleep somewhere. You can also keep an eye on him. If he needs to… If he needs anything, you'll have to help him anyway. Use a chamber pot for that because he'll never make it to the toilet, and keep a bucket ready in case he gets sick. Make sure there's also a glass of water because the poor soul will be thirsty."

"And what if he has something infectious?"

"Stefan, we live in four small rooms, if I can call the attic where the boys sleep a room. Adri's been here the whole evening. You caught him in your arms when he fainted and we helped him to bed. What good would it do to worry about getting sick now when the harm has probably already been done?" said the ever-practical Marije.

Stefan knew there was no choice but to accept her iron logic.

"Wake me up if you're worried about anything." She stood up to wash the milk beakers and make one last round through the house, while Stefan checked that he had properly closed the front door.

They kissed each other good night on the cheek and Marije giggled that this was the first time in ten years they wouldn't sleep in the same bed.

In the light of a small table lamp, Stefan undressed to his underwear and put on his pajamas, feeling extremely awkward, though he didn't quite understand why. If he considered everything he and Adri had done together, getting into bed with him solely to sleep was pure innocence.

She trusted him...

He tried to avoid touching the man beside him. He didn't want to disturb the much-needed sleep of the feverish man. But who was he fooling?

Adri moved restlessly, as if he were trying to find something.

"You're with us. You're very ill and you're staying until you get better." Stefan tried to be helpful, but Adri only looked more confused.

"You're safe with me. I promise."

"I feel so sick," Adri groaned and in a gesture of deep and honest compassion, Stefan took him in his arms and rocked his lover to sleep.

* * * *

The next morning, Marije decided it was better to ask Doctor Vriesema to look at Adri, whose condition had definitely worsened during the night. Vriesema, who had taken over the practice of Doctor De Jong after his retirement, examined the patient and shook his head. "I don't have to tell you this man is seriously ill. He has a lung and throat infection. I'll give you a prescription, but he'll need a lot of care and nursing over the next few days."

"That's no problem. He's welcome in our home as long as he needs it. He has no one else to take care of him," Marije said simply.

"Absolutely," Stefan added, though he knew his agreement was a formal one at best. The home and all it implied was his wife's domain, his duty in life was to support and provide.

"And no worries about the costs for medical care. I'll make sure it's taken care of one way or the other." Vriesema took another look at Adri, who looked more unconscious than peacefully asleep. "I'll come by later today."

Stefan put on his coat. "I'll get the medicines. You need anything else?"

"Don't forget your control stamp, because we can't do without the money right now." Marije took a scrap of paper and a pencil. "I'll write down what I need you to get. I know it's a bit farther away, but go to Pieters, because they're much cheaper than the public wash-house for soap and soda. And there's going to be a lot of extra sheets to wash."

For the first time, Stefan was almost grateful he was out of work after having been employed for a couple of months, even realizing that Adri's illness would mean a serious burden on the Doffer household finances. He couldn't pretend he cared about that. As long as his lover got better, he was prepared to forego the meatballs on Wednesday and eat kale and smoked sausage — without the sausage — for weeks to come. He would make sure the children had everything they needed, but all he needed was for his lover to be alive. He got the first stamp of that day, the medication, the groceries and even remembered to walk to Adri's current employer to tell him about the situation. At least he was able to do something of use.

The older children spent the hours after school with *Opoe* Doffer, to keep the house as quiet as possible, but even Ida understood that there was something very serious going on with her uncle. She walked on tiptoes and put her finger against her lips and said, "Ssssshhhhh," as loudly as possible whenever her mother as much as opened a cupboard to get out a cup.

For over a week, it took Stefan all his powers of persuasion to get Adri to drink some water, but he could swallow nothing more—not even a spoonful of white bread soaked in hot milk. There was little to do but sit at his side and watch his lover wrestle the enemy alone.

For modesty's sake he was the one giving Adri his daily sponge bath and, as much as he tried to see his friend's body as just like any other, inside him bewilderment screamed. How was it possible that this glorious body he had loved and possessed, and that had loved and possessed him in return, had become so thin and pale, so deathlike?

Several times a day, he took out the jug to help Adri pee. It soon enough became a routine, but the first time he held the man's penis, it was almost shocking in its intimacy. Deeper even was the shame of realizing how sad he felt because never before had his lover's male organ failed to harden under his touch.

Finally, the worst had passed when Adri accepted a few spoonfuls of broth, smiled then said, "Nice, thank you." Slowly over the following days, he ate porridge and soup, with a rusk with sugar as the absolute highlight.

A day later, he insisted on visiting the toilet instead of using the pot, and with unsteady legs, heavily leaning on Stefan, he began to regain his independence. He still slept for most of the day, but Stefan could tell that his dreams were becoming less fearful. How good it was to hear him breathing with ease, instead of the labored struggle to cling on to whatever life he had left in him.

"I think I'll be able to go home to my own place," Adri announced when he had managed to walk to the toilet, sit upright for an hour and eat a sandwich with fresh Gouda cheese.

Marije laughed. "How are you supposed to take care of yourself if you can't even keep yourself awake all day? You try to stay out of that bed for longer than a few hours then we'll talk."

"But I've been a burden to you for almost a month. I sleep in your bed, there's the extra laundry, the kids can't behave like real kids and I dread to think about the extra costs involved. I promise to pay back every cent as soon as I get a new job, because no boss keeps a man who's been ill for over a month when there are a hundred guys waiting in line to take his place."

"The doctor's bill has been taken care of, and the rest will take care of itself. With a family there's always laundry and a mouse eats more in a day than you have in the past few weeks." Marije walked to the kitchen. "Shall I make you some fresh tea? You want some too, Stefan?"

"Don't mind if I do." Stefan could whistle with happiness seeing Adri at the table, drinking a cup of tea, eating a biscuit. His friend was doing better by the day, even though he still couldn't stay awake after supper, and thus Marije told him to go to bed, because he obviously needed it.

He woke up for a moment when Stefan joined him, making sure everything was all right. Stefan kissed him gently on the forehead and they settled for the night.

"Why do you have to get sick enough to almost die before I can spend a night with you in my arms?" Stefan whispered, assuming Adri was already asleep.

Adri snuggled a little closer, as if he wanted to say it all didn't matter anymore. He had been lost in the twilight between life and death but had finally woken in the arms of his lover. In a few days, he would return to his own bed and everything would be back to the way it always had been, but they both knew they would carry these weeks, both the dark shadow of death and the joy of being alive, with them for the rest of their lives.

Adri took Stefan's hand in his own and drew it under the blankets.

Stefan understood the silent question. It surprised him, but it was a good surprise. His lover's cock became erect after a few strokes. How he had missed that sensation, the hard proof that his lover wanted him. He explored the miracle with curious fingers, followed the vein and fondled the scrotum, pulled down the foreskin. Slowly he masturbated the man he loved to completion, catching the soft moans with his own mouth. It was his celebration of life, his blessing.

"Thank you," Adri whispered, "for everything."

* * * *

More than ever Adri had become a part of the Doffer family. He shared dinner with them a few times a week and spent most Sunday afternoons in their living room. He played chess with Sientje, helped the boys with their jigsaw puzzles and visibly enjoyed Ida's enthusiastic stories about how she had petted the big black dog of the milkman.

Marije refused his money, and Stefan knew better than to contradict his wife in situations like that, so Adri settled the matter by putting a bag of assorted sweets on the table, a dozen eggs and four big, red, blushing apples. "I'm sure you can use this for your insatiable little monsters."

She just shook her head and smiled.

Later, after supper, Stefan asked him for their customary walk.

"I'm at a loss for what to do with myself," he started, when he had closed the door behind them. "As soon as I know you're spending an evening with us, I can't think of anything else but you."

Adri nodded his understanding. "And that makes you feel guilty."

"I can't make a right out of a wrong, even knowing we would be best mates anyway, because we're really and honestly best mates and I still want you. But on the days I can't meet you, it's as if I'm staring at a brick wall, feeling pity for myself."

"I feel so at home with your family, even though I know I should stay as far away as possible and I can't even kiss you on the cheek or hold you in my arms for a second without it looking suspicious. But there's no denying you're a good husband, Stefan Doffer. I would say yes if you'd asked me." Adri stopped walking and waited for a reaction.

"That's not a subject to make jokes about, Adri. It's downright improper for me to invite my — I'm not even sure what to call you — into my own household." Stefan tried his best to keep his voice low, but he couldn't stop himself from looking around nervously.

"I'm a guest as a friend of the family, not as your lover."

"As if it's possible to separate the one from the other," Stefan objected. "So often you sit across from me at the table and I truly don't understand why Marije doesn't see that I'm undressing you with my eyes."

"Perhaps because she can't imagine that sexual attraction as deep as it is between us even exists? Hasn't everything changed for you because you discovered it was possible to really lust after another human being, instead of performing your marital duties with someone who would rather show you she cares in any other way but that?" Adri paused. "You're no longer blind to the signs and so you have a hard time imagining others still walk around in the dark."

"You mean she doesn't recognize the look in our eyes because she's never looked that way at other people herself? If that's true, then what I do is all the more wrong because I'm cheating on someone who has no chance of defending herself," concluded Stefan.

Adri's calm voice betrayed hidden agitation. "Defend against what? If you'd been a free man, I would have conquered you and never let you go, make no mistake about that, but you're married and you'll stay married. I'm no threat to your family. If we stopped making love but continued as normal friends, would that make a difference?"

"Then you'd just be a friend."

"You prefer me to stay away from you?" Adri clearly wasn't about to pass the challenge.

"I'd still be cheating on my wife and breaking my marriage vow in thought. You were so ill and I feared you'd die, but every night I held you in my arms and imagined I was the one chasing away your nightmares." Stefan stared at the pavement under his feet. "It's hard for me to get used to no longer having you beside me in bed. It's her place and nothing will ever change that, but I miss you."

"The first night in my own bed I couldn't sleep. I enjoy eating at your table, sharing your meal, but I don't know how to get through the nights," Adri whispered, so softly that his words were hardly audible.

Stefan looked at him. Adri was cured of the lung infection but still not back to his full strength, and his emaciated face made it hard for Stefan to stop himself putting an arm around Adri's shoulder. For a moment he laid a hand on his lover's arm, but approaching footsteps made him hastily retract it. To conceal his unease, he lit a cigarette. He didn't know what was worse — the shame because he had almost been caught in a compromising situation with another man or the shame of brutally denying everything that connected him to the man he loved.

Chapter Thirteen

Stefan's world had always been a relatively small one, even before he'd married and started a family of his own. The minor amount of religious upbringing he had enjoyed boiled down to a vague idea that there must be something more, and he considered politics an activity for those who didn't have to work for a living. If he hadn't been in and out of a job on an irregular basis, the whole economic crisis would have gone right past him. Once a week he got a new book from Jakoba Huyzen's lending library, but he knew he probably wouldn't read a newspaper even if he were able to afford a subscription to one. He listened to popular music and plays on the radio, but got distracted when the news was on.

It wasn't easy to put himself in Adri's position, always wanting to know what was happening in the world. His friend never liked to miss any of the speeches from those in power, and he visited a few political rallies of different parties because he believed that not wanting to know was not an option. He had even toyed with the thought of going to Spain to fight against Franco, but the look in Stefan's eyes when he'd mentioned the idea had been enough to keep him safely home.

"I don't know if you're aware of what's happening in Germany, with Herr Hitler, but you only need to listen to a few stories from Jewish and political refugees and you know things will go wrong there. It's no longer a matter of if, but of when." Adri sat at the table across from Stefan.

Marije was checking on Wilfred, who had a bit of a cough. She wanted to make sure he wasn't developing a fever.

"We are here, in Holland, not in Germany." Stefan didn't like it when Adri rode his political high horse. Why worry about something you couldn't influence anyway? He had found another job for as long as it lasted, and there was hopeful talk going around that the worst was over and businesses and factories were hiring again. How it could have happened, with so many unemployed all over the world, had been mostly a riddle to him, but he wasn't one to ask questions. They paid the rent on time and Marije's housekeeping money allowed for slightly more expense than the family strictly needed just to stay alive.

"Anything there can visit us here." No, Adri wasn't about to give up on this easily. "You have to understand that this danger doesn't go away if we simply ignore it long enough."

"If you insist on talking politics, at least help me to understand." Stefan was starting to become seriously irritated with the whole matter. He wanted a nice, quiet evening with his best friend. Wasn't life hard enough as it was?

"Don't pretend you have no idea what's happening in Germany. They're building their army, Stefan, they're openly talking about needing more space for the German people." To accentuate his arguments, Adri moved his hands in large gestures.

"Yeah, Holland is just what they need if they want more space," sneered Stefan.

"The Port of Rotterdam, England's right across the sea. We're nothing but a stepping stone for them." Adri lit a cigarette.

"What's all the talk about? You men are becoming a bit loud. Please keep it down for the little ones," Marije intervened.

"Sorry, girl," apologized Stefan. "How's Wilfred doing?"

"He still has a bit of a cough but no fever, so he's going to be okay in a day or so." Marije put away the cups that were left on the table after the seven o'clock coffee. "Before I forget to tell you, I need more storage space in the kitchen."

"There are a few pieces of leftover wood at my work and I'll ask the boss if it's okay to use them. I can offer to do a few hours overtime for them as payment," Stefan promised.

"I think there's going to be a war," Adri said all of a sudden. The words sounded raw in the quiet little living room. "Okay, perhaps 'war' is too big a word."

But the damage was done. "That was what you were talking about, wasn't it? That was what the noise was about." Marije looked at him with fear in her eyes. "But we're neutral. The prime minister said so on the radio."

"You trust them, in Germany?" The question cut like a knife.

"I hear things, of course, when I go for groceries, but I can't imagine normal Germans, people like us, want war. Have they already forgotten the last one?" Marije shook her head. "You shouldn't talk like that. It's spoiling a nice evening."

"Tell that to the Jewish shopkeeper who lost everything and is just happy he's allowed to set up a little market stall in Amsterdam, or to the socialist union worker who just spent eight months in a labor camp for openly doubting the blessings of the Nazi party."

"Adri, stop preaching to my wife."

"I'm really sorry if I upset you, Marije, but looking away won't make it go away. You're right. I'm bad company at the moment. I apologize." Adri stood up, put on his coat and asked, "Take a walk around the block?"

Stefan stayed where he was. "No thanks."

"Have it your way. See you tomorrow in the park after work." And out he went.

* * * *

"I was angry yesterday, because you wouldn't listen, but I shouldn't have walked away like that," Adri admitted, sitting next to Stefan on the park bench.

"I couldn't move and I didn't know if it was because I was angry or because I was afraid I'd never see you again." Stefan didn't look at Adri while he continued to talk. "What do you see in me? I care so little for the things that interest you. You have friends who know about politics and art and other intellectual stuff, and they probably agree with you about what's happening in the world. Perhaps we should face the truth. Two men together, that's hard enough as it is, even without all the differences between us. It's a miracle it's lasted this long."

"We had a fight. That's all. Even friends sometimes disagree. Even special friends can have their bad days. I want you, Stefan Doffer, even if you hardly read a newspaper and only vote because its compulsory and you can't afford the fine."

"You have time to worry about politics, but I have other things on my mind." Stefan knew he was ignoring what Adri had tried to say about wanting him.

"Nice try. With or without a family, you don't care for politics and you have that right, even if I disagree with you and think it's a dangerous position." Adri moved his leg against Stefan's for a fleeting second. "I'm serious about wanting you. I walked home yesterday with those big angry strides because I didn't know what to do with myself, and I was afraid I was going to kick the first poor sod I came across. I was still worked up when I got to my room. It had nothing to do with politics, though. I really needed to make up with you."

"I thought we just did. Or are you still mad at me?"

Adri chuckled. "Not that kind of making up."

"I did spend a few extra minutes on the toilet before I went to bed," Stefan admitted. "I would have felt bad bothering Marije with that."

"At least I have a room of my own, with a comfortable bed and privacy." Adri grinned like a schoolboy admitting to a clever trick.

"Saturday afternoon we'll have an opportunity to be alone." Stefan stood right. "I have to hurry. Marije will be waiting with the potatoes."

"That's only three nights away. Go to your potatoes before they get cold." Adri was all but inaudible when he asked, "Care for a kiss?"

Stefan looked right, left and even behind him before he moved closer to Adri, and kissed him quickly on the lips. He walked away as fast as he could, afraid someone might have seen him.

* * * *

The whole afternoon was theirs. Marije and the kids were paying a birthday visit to an old school friend of Marije's, who was married herself and mother of three boys. She had even invited the Doffers to stay for supper, since she planned on making a big pot of vegetable soup and there would be more than enough for everyone.

"You honestly don't mind staying home? It's fine if you build that storage in the kitchen some other time. I honestly hadn't thought about..."

"To be honest, with the house empty, Adri and I can work faster. When you're back, your kitchen will look like new. Have fun, and I'll see you in the evening." Had he become shameless? He didn't feel shame — or did he?

"But what about supper for you?"

"I know I'm a man, but I believe I'm quite capable of making a couple of cheese sandwiches, and knowing Adri, he's probably been to the market to get some herring or sprat."

Within a few hours, the kitchen had improved considerably, with more storage space and a fresh coat of whitewash on the ceiling.

"She'll be ever so pleased with it." Stefan nodded, content with a job well done. "Thanks for the help."

"Looks good, doesn't it?" Adri, still in his overalls, cleaned his brush, washed his hands and turned around to Stefan, a big grin on his face. "Time for the next job."

"You promised your landlady? And it has to be today of all days? I thought we had a deal about this afternoon." It was impossible for Stefan to hide his disappointment. It took him a few seconds before he understood why Adri burst out laughing and instead of hastening to his landlady's house, started to undress. Still blushing with embarrassment, he followed his lover's example.

Lovemaking was relaxed and pleasant, worthy of a free afternoon with enough privacy to enjoy the luxury of time. When they were sated with love, they stayed closely connected, not yet ready for the inevitable physical separation.

"I could do this for the rest of my life, work with you and make love with you and stay in your arms until the end of time," Adri sighed happily.

"I'm sorry," Stefan apologized.

"For giving me a couple of wonderful hours that will get me through the next week?" Adri moved his hand over Stefan's chest and belly, and lower. "What a thing of beauty it is, a man's body."

"You never felt the same for a woman? I mean, you always considered a woman's body a dirty thing?" Stefan tried to ignore his hardening cock, because he really wanted an answer to his question.

"I'm not blind to a sweet face or a nice body, but it doesn't do much for me if it's a female one. I wouldn't say women are dirty to me. I just prefer the company of men in my bed." Adri teased Stefan's pubic hair.

"What is it about a man that excites you so much that you're willing to take this many risks and you're even prepared to give up any hope of a normal and happy life?"

Adri frowned, but continued to explain. "I could spend a whole day simply summing up everything about you that I like. Your red hair totally does it for me. With your hands, you touch me and that tells me so much. Do you realize how weak in the knees I get when you roll up your sleeves on a warm summer's day? How there's a sudden army of butterflies in my belly when I'm sitting on the park bench and I see you walking toward me?"

"You too? Weeks before I recognized what was happening between us, I started to get a strange feeling every time I saw you. And I've felt it ever since."

Adri kissed him. "I mustn't forget to tell you about your eyes and your mouth, or that special place on your neck I always want to kiss whenever I see it. You like it when I tease your nipples. Your breathing goes faster when I caress your inner thigh, even if you're still wearing your trousers."

"Looks like you know more about me than I do about myself." Stefan's surprise wasn't feigned. He honestly wasn't able to envision how or why another man could see his body the way Adri did and how his body reacted to his lover's words.

"You've got an arse to kill for and when you stoop to get something from the ground, I have to stop myself from copping a feel," Adri whispered into Stefan's ear and his fingers circled around the now painfully hard erection. "I won't speak about your cock, because anything I say will be too much and still not enough."

Stefan was hyperaware of his lover's gaze, of the visible signs of his body's desire. He had never felt this naked, without protection. He closed his eyes to hide his vulnerability. Not a word was spoken while Adri's hand pumped up and down in a perfect rhythm. He groaned his pleasure against his lover's shoulder. Then it was over.

Not having any other choice he looked up and with every ounce of tenderness he had in him, leaned toward his lover and kissed the tears from his eyes.

* * * *

He frowned when Adri pushed the book into his hands. "What's it about?"

"What it says on the cover, it's about people like us — homosexuals. Not just about us, but people like us telling how it feels."

"Us? I'm not a homosexual. I just love you. What am I supposed to do with this?"

"Read it. What else?" Adri sounded like he was losing his patience. "You have any idea how much trouble Jakoba went through to find this? To even know it existed in the first place?"

"You know damn well I'm not interested in books like this. It has absolutely nothing to do with me." Stefan knew there was a storm brewing, but why did Adri keep on insisting he should be interested in matters that left him cold and indifferent?

"It has to do with me and with us, and for that reason alone you should take the trouble." Why didn't he just give up?

Stefan put the book on the table, pushed it away. "I just happen to have fallen in love with you, nothing more."

"You just happen to be a man who has fallen in love with another man."

"That's bad enough as it is, but do they have to bother decent people with their abnormality?"

Adri drummed with his fingers on the book. He squeezed his eyes in anger.

Stefan laughed in disdain. "No, you have to be proud of it."

"These aren't happy stories of happy people, Stefan. No one in this book is proud of what they are, but they had the courage to speak up, even in anonymity, because they hope normal people might think a little better of them and because it might make men like us — me — feel a little less alone. Not everyone has friends like the ones I meet at Jo's," Adri sighed. "Not everyone has you."

"I'll read it. Promise."

"You want something back for doing that?"

"I said I'll read it."

"I'll take it home."

"Leave it."

"And Marije?"

"It won't be the first thing I've had to keep away from her."

"You're right. I shouldn't have brought the book here." Adri picked it up from the table. "Just because I share my body with you, doesn't mean—"

"It's no use pretending I don't care about you, is it? You're my friend, and if something is important to you, I can't say I don't want to know about it and still call myself a friend. Leave the book here, and next week I'll tell you what I think about it."

"Are you going to start reading right away, or will you have time for something else first?" Adri stood up, walked over to Stefan and kissed him on the mouth. "Well...?"

* * * *

"I tried to read it, but I couldn't finish it."

"Too uncomfortable?"

"You're disappointed?"

Adri pulled him tighter into his arms.

"You had a good time at Jo's?"

Adri looked genuinely surprised at Stefan's interested inquiry. "Yeah, and I had a good laugh too. Someone had been to America and he had met someone who knew a doctor who was sure a man's body actually betrays that he's doing it with other men."

"Well, if they're a bit effeminate, it's easy enough to spot."

"That's not what that doctor was referring to. No, he was certain that if he shoved a stick down someone's throat, a normal man would show a normal gag response and a homosexual wouldn't."

Stefan scratched his head before he started to grin. "I get it. You're pulling my leg. Nice try, Adri, nice try."

"You have no idea how serious I am, although I have to admit this one is kind of funny. We don't have a gag reflex, the proportions of our shoulders-to-hips ratio is more like that of a woman and hell, even our arses refuse to behave in a normal, manly way!" Adri laughed.

Stefan couldn't help joining him, only to suddenly fall silent again. "Why are we laughing?"

"Why shouldn't we? People will make up the most blatant nonsense rather than admit that sex between two men is just that, sex between two men. You don't need anything special for that."

"It might be helpful if you're actually attracted to men before you bed one."

"Why else would we be here, naked and all? To upset the normal order, even if we hate what we're doing?" Adri chuckled. "In my eyes you're the most attractive man I've ever laid eyes on, even if I know there are many more handsome men walking this earth. I get happy just knowing you exist, and you get one chance to guess how my body reacts when I'm near you."

"I don't have to guess that." Stefan groped between Adri's legs.

"Trying to distract me from a serious conversation about a serious subject?"

"No, trying to see if you're up for another round before your landlady gets home." Stefan bowed his head over his lover's erection and gave a playful lick over the full length.

"Going to test your gag reflex?" Adri teased.

Stefan looked up and smiled. "No, going to make love to you the best I can."

Minutes later, he held a sated lover in his arms. He didn't want to talk just yet, but he understood why Adri had asked him if he honestly enjoyed what he did, sucking on a dick and even swallowing.

"I wouldn't do it if I didn't enjoy it. I'm not married to you, so there's no duty."

"Is your life about duty?"

"Isn't that the case for most people?"

"Even if that duty makes you sick and miserable? Even if you have to pretend?"

"I'm not miserable. I'm a normal, married man with a family, and I'm convinced you can have exactly the same if only you'd give it a serious try."

Adri kissed him deeply. "Your mouth tastes of my sperm."

Touché.

"Perhaps there are two kinds of men doing it with other men? Those who are more like women and the other ones."

"And we just happen to be the other ones?"

"You're angry at me for saying that?"

"No. Perhaps I should be, but I'm not."

"I don't understand it. Why do some men have needs like this? What's the use if it only brings shame, rejection and loneliness? And it must be a strong need, or why would I even take the risk?"

"Most psychiatrists consider it an illness. Simply explained, you have the body of a man but the longings of a woman."

"One that can be cured?"

Adri pushed his nose against Stefan's neck and inhaled deeply. "I rather enjoy my medical condition."

"But if it's true about men like us being more like women, why did I never in my life have the inclination to play hopscotch or learn to knit?"

"Perhaps because for some men it is true that they have the soul of a woman and the body of a man? But that's just some men — and all the others, men like us, are getting ignored, so the doctors don't have to admit that we're not much different from normal men."

"Even without feeling like a woman, a real man doesn't allow another man to take him from behind." Stefan knew exactly what he was saying.

"Then tell me to be passive in bed. I enjoy taking you as much as being taken by you, but if it bothers you that much, I'll get on my belly for you and take it like a man."

"That's not what I mean."

"I know."

"What I do is wrong, no matter which way I look at it."

"What about outsiders staying out of the bedrooms of consenting adults?"

"I'm a married man and a father."

"You didn't know."

Was that an excuse for what he had done? Stefan didn't even dare to ask the question.

Chapter Fourteen

It was easy enough for Adri to come up with the brilliant idea of borrowing the beach cottage of one of the friends he had met at Jo Swart's house, but Stefan couldn't just stay away for the night — not even if Marije went for a weekend to her parents, taking the children with her. He was simply expected to join them.

"Please, Stefan, we'll have a whole afternoon and evening and night and morning together. Compare that with a few minutes here, a few hours there. It's outside the summer season, so imagine the privacy." Adri wasn't about to give up easily. He opened a few buttons of Stefan's undershirt and caressed his chest. "A day and a night, a bed and a room with a lock."

Stefan sighed with equal excitement and regret. "It's impossible."

Adri twitched a nipple between his thumb and index finger. "Can't — or won't?"

"Ouch. That's not a fair question, and you know it. I can't find a believable excuse to avoid going to my parents-in-law. Besides, they're good people."

Perhaps more than trying to explain to Adri why he really couldn't go to that cottage, Stefan was trying to silence his need to be with his lover.

"I'll tell my friend we won't be able to make use of his kind offer," Adri said. "The facts are what they are, aren't they? And with a bit of luck we can rent a room some place for an hour or so. That's something, at least." To show he wasn't mad at Stefan, he got on his knees and opened his friend's corduroy trousers.

The idea stayed in his head and refused to budge. Ever since Adri had been so ill and they had slept in the same bed for several weeks, not a day had passed when he didn't long for that time. Simply knowing his lover was sleeping peacefully beside him would be enough. After three days, he made the decision.

* * * *

"I'm not sure if I'm a really bad person or just love you too much, but I told some ugly lies to be with you in that cottage in the dunes," he said to Adri while they were waiting for the train that would take them to the coast. "I'm getting used to keeping things from her, telling only half of the story, but this…"

"You have about twenty-four hours to decide if it was worth the guilt."

"I told her I had to stay home because the money for the train would be too much and her parents wouldn't miss me as long as she and the grandchildren were there. She kept saying she'd saved money for the train for all six of us and her parents would be so disappointed. I reminded her that our eldest girl was going to need a new winter coat in a few months' time. So now she thinks I'm the perfect father."

"Well, at least there's no discussion about that," Adri said. "Or you'd have run away with me and never looked back."

"Leaving Marije to fend for herself and her four children, all under the age of ten, in a time where even family men have a hard time finding a job—and all because I happened to meet a handsome young man? Absolutely not."

"You wouldn't be the man I fell in love with. Besides, it's fun being an unofficial uncle to your kids." Adri smiled at Stefan. "But here's the train."

* * * *

They had to walk for almost an hour from the tiny station to the vacation home, which was plenty of time for Stefan to get used to the idea that he was about to spend a night with a very healthy Adri.

The tiny cottage had walls made of sand-colored wood, a red roof, a green door and window frames, with the red-and-white checkered curtains closed. It was almost unreal in its doll-like cuteness.

"Let's take a look inside, but be careful or you'll scare the fairies and gnomes." Adri laughed, turning the key to open the front door.

Stefan couldn't help smiling when he saw the small table and two wicker chairs, a sink with a cold-water tap, a cupboard and a gas burner. He opened the cupboard and found Bakelite tableware, cutlery and an assortment of candles, an oil lamp, canned food, coffee and sugar.

"The bedroom is that way," Adri whispered in his ear. "Give the bed a try before I make coffee and a few sandwiches?"

Stefan grinned and pushed Adri inside the bedroom and onto the bed. He landed right on top of his lover, kissing him greedily, groping his arse with both hands, grinding their erections together through the fabric of two sets of trousers and underpants.

"You have spare clothes with you?" Adri managed to say.

"Huh? What? Damn…"

Hastily, and perhaps somewhat clumsily, they undressed and continued where they had left off. No refinement, they were just two men groping and grinding until they ended in a sweaty, sated embrace.

Adri stretched and yawned. "Are you hungry? Then you'll have to let go of me so I can get us some food. There's bread, cheese and I think I saw a can of corned beef."

Less than ten minutes later they sat at the table with a huge pile of sandwiches between them and ate in amicable silence.

"I'm really famished after that walk from the station," Stefan said innocently, taking a bite from his fourth sandwich. "What are you laughing about?"

"Absolutely nothing." Adri grinned. "What about a walk before it gets dark?"

In the absence of the day-trippers from summer, the beach looked quiet and deserted, with just the endless sound of the waves coming and going. Stefan saw no need to add his voice to that of the sea, and was grateful Adri seemed to be in the same mood. He watched the sun disappearing like a pale orange ball into the dark gray of endless water, and without touching or looking, he knew his lover was close by. He wasn't a man to get lyrical about sunsets, but the reason for being there made his heart pound. The universe had tried everything in its power to keep them apart, yet they stood next to each other on the beach to see the onset of darkness.

Adri nudged him from his motionless stance. In blind trust he walked behind his friend, not having a real idea exactly where they were or in which direction they were going. Suddenly, as they walked between two rows of dunes, Adri stopped and gestured to Stefan to keep very quiet.

Stefan could still hear the sound of the sea from afar, and closer, the sound of the wind through the marram grass. Then, with a sudden shock, there was another sound and he knew what it was, although he didn't want to see it with his own eyes. He didn't want to look into that mirror, but it was impossible not to look.

The boys — they couldn't have been much more than sixteen — were too preoccupied with each other to notice anything around them. It was evening, in a hollow in the dunes away from the path, and the last summer guest had gone home weeks ago. Stefan understood why they had forgotten the vigilance which he knew to be already a firm part of their behavior. And yet he experienced no negative emotions in observing the youthful embrace, only a vague sadness for chances missed.

Back in the cottage, Adri lit the oil lamp, made tea and peeled a few apples. The everyday reality of the scene moved Stefan. He knew his lover in a way that shocked most people to the core of their bones, but seldom did they have the chance to offer each other the simple gestures that were so much more a part of marriage than passion. To his own surprise, he longed as much to drink tea and eat apples together as he did for the joining of their bodies. No matter what Adri told him about doctors and lawyers writing that the love between men was immature and fleeting, if he had known then what he knew now, he would have postponed leaving his parents' home until his lover was old enough to set up a household with him. It was an unrealistic dream, but for once he didn't fight it.

"Sweet, those boys, don't you think?" Adri voiced their shared feeling of endearment.

"Sometimes it's hard to remember how it was, being that young. Having those strange thoughts that made you want to touch yourself, knowing it was wrong and doing it anyway," Stefan said wistfully. "And you?"

"Waiting for you and knowing it too, without ever being fully aware of it until I actually met you. If you'd been a bit younger and I a bit older, I would have eloped with you the day before your wedding if that was what it took." Adri grinned impishly, then became serious again. "Now it will never be possible for me to peel potatoes while you clean vegetables after work. Don't get me wrong, I'd like to make love with you every single day if we had a bed and privacy, but if that's all we'll ever share as a couple, my happiness will be incomplete. I'm envious of your wife, because she gets to take care of you and I don't."

"It wasn't easy for me to accept that I was able to have sex with a man, let alone that I would want it as much as I do, but it's almost harder to accept how much I love it when a man makes sandwiches for me or I get him another cup of tea. When I decided to join you instead of my family this weekend, I was looking forward to spending as much time in bed as possible, just doing one thing. I never took into account how happy it would make me, sitting at a table with you, pretending we're a real couple." Stefan ate the last part of the apple. He looked from the weak light of the oil lamp to his lover's face.

A tiny house, some bread and apples and an oil lamp were all he needed to be happy. And even though he was all too aware that the small space would soon enough create its own problems, and bread and oil cost money, it didn't diminish the simple truth of the matter. He had made a promise to his family and he would honor it to his very last breath, but he longed with all his heart to share his life with the man whose face he studied. It was a pleasant, open face, clear and honest. Stefan never needed to guess if a storm was brewing or if he was thinking about something funny. He certainly didn't need to guess if his lover was in the mood for sex.

Adri stood up, put the cups, plate and knife in the sink, cleaned them and put them away in the cupboard. He closed the curtains, undressed and washed his whole body with great care. "The water's bit cold, but it's not too bad." He took the oil lamp in his hand. "I want to see you and you to see me."

"I'd better follow your good example then."

The bedroom was about half the space of the already-small living room, with a three-quarter bed, a night table and a small wardrobe taking up almost every centimeter available. Adri placed the oil lamp on the table. "I bought a brand new tin of Vaseline. Wait. I'll get it."

"You do me?"

"Would you like that?"

"Yes." Stefan got on all fours, because he didn't know of a better way to show he wanted his lover with an urgent and absolute need. He was grateful that Adri's preparations were thorough but didn't take longer than was absolutely necessary to make penetration virtually painless. The groan he muffled against the pillow was one of pleasure.

"No one can hear us," Adri reminded him. "You're in pain?"

Too used to the absolute necessity of having sex with as little sound as possible, Stefan shook his head before he found the courage to open his mouth. Getting on his hands and knees to offer his body to his lover was relatively easy in comparison with giving voice to the overwhelming emotions he felt.

Without warning Adri slipped out of him.

"Please, don't do that."

"I just want you to turn on your back, so I can see your face."

With his legs clutched around his lover's middle, he surrendered to the night without a trace of fear. Nothing could threaten him, because he had become untouchable.

In the early-morning light they fell asleep from pure exhaustion. Later they ate breakfast and returned to the three-quarter bed once more to pretend that they wouldn't be waiting for the train home in less than two hours. They made love.

"I shouldn't have allowed you to persuade me to spend the night with you here," Stefan said, while he quickly looked around to make sure he hadn't forgotten anything before he and Adri left for the station.

Adri looked at him in sad confusion.

Stefan put his hand on his lover's shoulder. "We can't always be together. In fact, we can almost never be together like we were this weekend. I can't miss what I never had, but now that I actually know what it is, I'll be longing for it every single day of the rest of my life."

"I'm so sorry. I thought this would give us at least a day and a night of happiness."

Stefan took Adri into his arms. "It did make me happy. Don't you understand that this happiness is what makes me so unhappy?"

Silently they walked to the station, silently they sat in the train to the city, and silently Adri accompanied Stefan to his front door.

"See you tomorrow night, after work?"

Stefan opened the door and nodded. Of course they would see each other. Was there a reason to break their usual routine?

"You're going to laugh at me, but I kept count of the last couple of days. Including everything from the moment we stepped into that cottage until that last quickie before we had to go, we did it a dozen times." Adri chuckled. "Can you believe it?"

Stefan couldn't stop himself from laughing.

"Twelve times in barely twenty-four hours? We're a real couple of horny dogs."

Adri looked up the stairs. "Nobody's home, or else your boys would have stormed down. Close the door and we'll make it a baker's dozen."

Chapter Fifteen

Despite Adri's almost obsessive warnings about what was happening in Germany and the invasion of Poland in August 1939, Stefan read their mobilization papers, shaking his head in disbelief. He thought about his family, about the fact that Marije would have to make do again with far less money than he had started to earn once more.

"I'm getting kicked back just when I thought we'd finally made it past the years of poverty. It's almost like a huge hand is pushing me down into the mud, no matter how hard I work."

But more than his concern for his family, there was the knowledge that he and Adri would have their army quarters too far from each other to make visits a realistic possibility. Their love, almost fully depending on Adri spending a few nights a week as a guest with Stefan and his family, stolen minutes at the bottom of the stairs and whatever hours of privacy they managed to scrape together, wouldn't have a chance against a separation which would last an unknown period of time.

"I'll find a way to see you," Adri told him. "I promise."

Stefan put his mobilization card into the pocket of his jacket, knowing that the definite end of their love would arrive in the form of a short letter. Adri would write to him about another man, one he didn't have to share with a wife and four children, and that would be the end of it.

* * * *

"I missed you so much." Adri kissed again and again, his arms firmly around Stefan, whose body reacted with immediate urgency. Adri understood his need, likely because it was his own, and led him to the bed.

They had met in a small hotel halfway between their army camps. A simply decorated room with a clean bed was to be their home and kingdom for a few hours.

"You still believe there's going to be a war?" Stefan asked.

"The war is already there. We just have to wait until it's our turn."

"We've been mobilized for half a year now and nothing's happening. Perhaps the Germans are too busy in Poland and they'll pass us by and go straight to Belgium and France, like in 1914." Stefan was talking his worries away.

Adri nodded. "Feel free to believe that."

Stefan stood up from the bed and looked through a split between the curtains. "It's hard to imagine anyone's in for a war, with spring starting for real now. I want to go back to my family so I can decently provide for them and have you near me. Now and again you'll stay for supper or be alone with me on a Sunday afternoon, or we'll borrow a new book at Huyzen's or have a walk in the park—if need be, with both boys and Ida to keep us company."

Adri stretched out his hand. "It's all been long decided, Stefan. We can only react after the event, and that won't matter much either."

Stefan joined him once more on the bed. "I have a family. How am I supposed to feel about this? You're a man alone."

"I'm not a man alone," Adri said. "My heart will break if you die."

Stefan suddenly knew what he wanted to ask. "But I won't be leaving you unprotected and without a provider. That's why I want to ask you for a favor."

"I'll be there for your family the best I can. If I have food on the table, then so will they. As long as I have a pair of hands, they won't be without someone to look out for them. Marije has shown me nothing but friendship. I see your kids growing up and they're like family to me. More than that, they're part of you."

"You sound like you guessed what I was going to ask before I even asked the question," Stefan wondered aloud.

"You're surprised about that?" Adri closed his eyes and passively accepted Stefan's caresses. "I don't want to live with the thought of your death."

"There won't be a war, and one day we'll be old and gray and we'll still spend the occasional Sunday afternoon in bed," Stefan said decidedly. "I don't want to hear about you dying. So, tell me, what part of my body do you want to use for your pleasure?"

It would all be like the Great War that their parents had known. That hadn't been an easy time, with mobilization and trade restrictions, but no son, father or husband had marched to the battlefield and no enemy soldiers had threatened the women and children left behind.

"You'll write to me?" Stefan asked when they were ready to leave the hotel room. "But please, keep it discreet."

"You'll be able to show them to your mother-in-law. That's how neat and tidy my letters will be," Adri promised. "Although you don't know what you're missing. I can do a mean dirty letter if I set my mind to it."

"That's exactly why I asked you to keep it clean," Stefan chuckled. "Wait a few minutes. That way no one will see us together."

Two weeks later, Stefan heard and saw the planes which put an end to his hope that war would never happen.

* * * *

Stefan walked up the stairs with slow, dragging feet. The battle to defend their country against the German invasion had taken all of five days and the sacrifice of human life had been in vain. The Germans had bombed Rotterdam, completely destroying the center of the city, and the commander-in-chief of the Dutch army had signed the capitulation to prevent even worse. The royal family had fled abroad. No one and nothing now stood between his family and the enemy. Even stronger than the gnawing worry about Marije and the children, however, was the ceaseless hammering uncertainty of not knowing where Adri was and whether he was okay. His lover's death would mean a chance to return to normality, and that thought scared him.

Marije stood in the doorway, the children right behind her. If the German occupation was going to change everything in the coming months, this one moment was full of joy. He had made it home to see his family alive and healthy.

Stefan went inside and there he saw Adri, dressed in a uniform with visible signs of battle, sitting on the familiar chair at the table.

"Oh, my dear boy, you survived." Before he realized what was doing, Stefan was standing in the middle of the room, holding Adri in his arms.

"I had to know whether you'd made it," Adri whispered. "Oh God…"

They all sat around the table, chatting happily about how they were all together, but, at the same time, silently worried about the uncertain future.

* * * *

The Germans, for the most part, stayed invisible. Stefan was welcomed back to work with the same boss and heard that Adri hadn't had any trouble finding a job. Life returned to normal, as if the war had passed them by after all.

Just like before, Marije went to *Opoe* Doffer on a Sunday afternoon, taking the children with her. She visited other family members, too, and old school friends. Sometimes Stefan joined them. Sometimes he stayed at home and asked Adri if he felt like a game of chess.

He sat in one of the only two armchairs in the house. He had spent many evenings and Sundays on them, listening to the radio or reading detective novels. He had made the chairs in the months when he had been engaged to be married. He had chosen the wood, the upholstery and had put all his knowledge, care and countless free hours into those chairs.

Marije and the children were visiting cousin Lenie, who lived on the other side of the park. "It's such a nice walk. You really don't feel like joining us?"

"You know how Lenie's husband and I don't really get along. I have a nice book to read, and perhaps Adri will drop by. Don't worry about supper. I'll peel the potatoes for you. Say hi to everyone from me?"

He sat in the chair he had built with his own hands, his legs wide and his trousers loose. Adri was kneeling before him, staring intently at the forming erection. They hadn't kissed, hadn't touched, hadn't talked. It simply happened.

When Adri moved his head lower, Stefan didn't close his eyes as usual but decided to watch. He observed the scene with a slight astonishment. This was him, in his own chair, on a Sunday afternoon, and this was his best friend.

"Why?" he had to ask.

It took Adri a few seconds to register the question. "Why?"

"Why are you doing this?"

"You don't want it?"

"I do, but why are you doing this?"

"There's nothing to explain, is there? So please, let me continue." Adri sounded slightly worried and very impatient.

Yet for some reason Stefan found it harder to surrender to the pleasure brought about by his lover's mouth than usual. "She would never do this. She'd feel humiliated if I even suggested it."

"What are you going on about?" Adri frowned, obviously having no idea what was happening. "We have an afternoon all to ourselves, you get a hard-on before I've even touched you with a single finger, I'm in the mood to spoil you…and now this."

"I was watching you doing me and suddenly I couldn't get it out of my head — the why of what you're doing. I'm sorry. It's not much of an explanation, is it?" Stefan sighed in deep regret at what he was throwing away. "I have no idea why, but I need to know."

"Then I'll try to explain, although I won't be any clearer with words than with my body." Adri leaned his head against Stefan's thigh. "Funny how you're still hard."

"Can't help that."

"Long before I met you, I knew I wanted a man instead of a woman, and when I saw you, I realized almost from the start that it had to be you. I wanted to be with you, touch you and kiss you. I knew you would be in serious trouble with the law because of my age, so I counted the days until my birthday. Your body made me curious about my own, and about what's possible between us." Adri sighed. "That's not really an answer, is it?"

Stefan moved his hand from his lover's neck to his face, found his mouth and gently pushed three of his fingers past the lips. "I want to get lost inside you." He whispered the hopeless words.

Slowly Adri moved backward and looked at Stefan. "You answered your own question." One by one he kissed Stefan's fingers. "Your hands are so cold."

"Asking the question is one thing, admitting you already know the answer is something else. Are you never afraid?"

"Of losing you and finally settling for someone who will never be you, yes. Of losing myself in you? Why would I? I will never become part of you, whether I want that or not." Adri kissed the palm of Stefan's hand.

"I have a good wife. I made four children with her, two boys and two girls." Stefan sat motionless in his chair.

"I'll go home if you like."

Stefan shook his head in disbelief. "Why would you go home? You're with me."

"I want you and I'm not ashamed of that, even if I have to go against everything that's said and written," Adri said calmly.

"You changed my life with the first words you said to me."

Adri stood up, and now towered above Stefan. "I can't seduce you to something that's truly alien to you."

Half in panic Stefan stretched out his hand. "Please don't go."

"You trust me?" asked Adri.

Stefan nodded unthinkingly.

"You trust me enough to believe that I'll never allow you to do anything to me that I truly don't want. That I'll tell you to stop as soon as I've had enough?"

Stefan nodded again.

"Then get up from your chair and I'll show you what I plan to do. And lose the trousers. You don't want them to get in the way."

Stefan expected him to get on the chair himself or to take his hand and lead him to the bedroom, but instead Adri sat down on the floor, his back against the seat. He had no idea what would be expected of him, but he had promised his trust and that still counted for something.

"Straddle me, lean your knees against the edge of the chair and try out the most comfortable way to keep your balance while you — you know — move."

Suddenly Stefan saw the picture in his head. "I'll choke you that way. It's wrong. You can't ask this of me."

"I really want to try it. If it doesn't work for you the way I hope it will, or if it's too much for me, we'll do something else. You've already taken the biggest risk of your life, haven't you, just by kissing another man?" Adri leaned his head back as far as possible. "Please?"

In awe of his lover's courage and vulnerability, Stefan slowly and carefully pushed the head of his cock past Adri's lips, farther still, fully concentrating on even the slightest sign of discomfort. He looked down and saw that Adri had closed his eyes in deep surrender. There wasn't a trace of anxiety in his calm breathing in and out.

"Oh God," he sighed and he started to thrust fully in, completely out, faster and rougher than he thought he had the heart for, finally reaching his climax deep inside his lover's throat.

He took Adri into his arms and asked him if everything was okay.

"Don't I look okay?" The smile on his lover's face pretty much said it all.

Stefan lit up a cigarette and gave Adri the first puff. "But you want things that are strange and perhaps even dangerous."

"Strange is only strange because you haven't been told it's possible, and some things are more dangerous in your imagination than they are in reality."

"I admit it felt good, using your throat like that, but what's in it for you?"

"That's easy to answer — the pleasure of surrendering to your pleasure."

"I wouldn't have the courage. That I know for sure."

"Courage? I'm a man without any recognized ties, following his nature. You're risking your whole existence for something you had no idea about before you met me."

"It just happened, and I try to balance my life between two rights that are also two wrongs. I'm not even sure what I mean by that, so please don't ask. I don't have the courage either to walk away from you and never return or to leave Marije and the children for you. No, for all the big talk I talk about being a real man..." Stefan shrugged.

"Perhaps, one day, what is only for the rich, the crazy and the bohemians will be possible for ordinary folks as well."

"Yeah, right."

"It'll take about a hundred years, but you know that once we would have been jailed or even executed for what I'm about to ask from you? Now we're only expected to be over the age of twenty-one and to feel enough guilt and remorse for being what we are to prevent as much happiness as possible in men like us...me." Adri took Stefan's hand and led it to his still fully erect cock.

"And what are you asking me to do?"
"Use your imagination?"

Chapter Sixteen

"Stefan," Marije started and her voice had a certain tone, the one that told him she had taken her decision on an important matter and she expected him to follow her lead, even while pretending that he was in fact, in his role as head of the household, the one who had the veto. "We visit your mother as often as possible and you must have seen the same thing as I have. *Opoe* can't live alone any longer."

"What if we visit even more, every day if need be?" Stefan tried, against his better judgment.

"Shame on you, Stefan Doffer, even to suggest that there's no place in our home for your mother," Marije reprimanded him. "What if she's alone and she falls? And how am I supposed to be in two places at once? Do you expect Sientje to look after Selle and Wilfred after school while I cook *Opoe's* supper? And you can safely bet that Ida will be the boys' most trusted accomplice for any amount of mischief."

"That would be asking for disaster," Stefan admitted. "You're right. Mother's health has been declining for the past few months and it's impossible to run two households, one with four children and one with an invalid elderly person, both at the same time. Of course she's welcome in our home."

Within a week *Opoe* Doffer's bed stood in the girls' bedroom, and Marije somehow managed to find a place for her modest belongings as well. It also meant that Ida's bed returned to her parents' bedroom, because moving her in with her brothers was out of the question.

Opoe's health prevented her from doing more than a few odd jobs like peeling potatoes and cleaning Brussels sprouts, or keeping an eye on the boys while Marije made the rounds for groceries — an increasingly complicated job with most of what the family needed only available with coupons from their ration books.

Adri never complained to Stefan that the already scarce Sunday afternoons when the house was all theirs for a few hours were no longer possible. He simply rented a room with a bed and a door with a lock. He still joined the family dinner a few times a week, but more often than not he disappeared right after the seven o'clock coffee — or, rather, chicory — because he had business elsewhere. He never looked angry. He always walked away with a smile for everyone, but something had changed, and Stefan didn't have the courage to ask if this time it really was the beginning of the end.

* * * *

The children were all in bed, and *Opoe* followed not long after them. This was the only hour of the day when Stefan and Marije had any privacy.

"Marije, do you love me?"

It was the first time in his marriage he had asked her this question, because it was the first time he had wondered about it. Until his meeting with Adri, he had assumed it was all pretty much okay, that her life moved along with the same kind of contentment as his own. He had tried looking into her face once when he was having intercourse with her, not long after their first girl had been born, but he had seen the same calm expression she always wore when she was busy doing something she didn't particularly care for, but which did not fill her with revulsion either. Marital duty was part of the job, nothing more and nothing less. She lived for her children, for the pride of being able to send them to school with a full belly and a clean set of clothes, for the gentle praise and the sharp "Boys…" for the kisses on scraped knees and the patient untangling of unruly red hair. If Stefan were no longer there, she would grieve for him, but it wouldn't destroy her. On the other hand, the death of one of their – her – children would damage her beyond recognition.

He assumed she had become accustomed to him being part of her life, and that up to a point she honestly cared about him. She appreciated him as a father and a provider, but as man and a lover, he left her indifferent at best. He no longer believed that it was shyness which prevented her expressing the more basic needs that lived deep inside her. A warm heart beat inside her curvaceous body, but he had never seen even a hint, a subtle indication, of the blind, greedy lust that still overwhelmed him whenever he saw Adri.

Would it have made a difference, or would he still have fallen for a man anyway? Marije wasn't responsible for what had happened between Adri and him. It had nothing to do with her. She would have stood a more than reasonable chance against another woman, but this time she was powerless. Part of him wanted to tell her everything, finally come clean with her, at least give her a chance to defend what was still salvageable of their marriage, but he knew he would never actually say the words. He wasn't even sure if it was her he wanted to spare — or himself.

Was it possible she had no idea, even if that idea might well be far from the truth? Perhaps she thought all married men had their little secrets, the same way he assumed she had hers as well. They would remain strangers to each other, strangers who had found common ground in their love for their children and their appreciation for what each of them brought to the household. He accepted the fact of their marriage, and the knowledge that it would only end with the death of either of them, without a trace of self-pity. He also couldn't imagine she would leave him because of Adri, so why tell her?

She looked up from her needlework. "I'm sorry. I was lost in thought. You wanted to ask me something?"

"Do you love me?"

"We've been married for years. We have a family."

"That's not what I asked."

"You work hard for us. You're good to the children and me. What more could I ask of you?"

"When we were first married, did you have butterflies in your stomach?" How to put this in words? "What do you feel when you see me?"

"You're not an unattractive man, and I've always been proud to be seen with you," Marije said calmly as she snipped the thread of the mended shirt. Suddenly her movement froze and the expression on her face became sad and helpless. "Oh...you mean... Well, you know what you mean. You're trying to say you're not happy with me? I know the house is full and everything has become so complicated with the Germans being here and all, but if you want to, I can try to be a better wife. We can...have relations, when the children are at school. Perhaps when your mother has her afternoon nap you might come home from your job an hour, for lunch? You're working in the neighborhood at the moment, aren't you?"

He shook his head. "No, you're the mother of my children and I'm not going to use you like that. Not when it doesn't make you happy."

"I'm not giving you what you need as a man, am I?"

He knew he wasn't being fair to her, because no matter whether he told her the truth or tried to spare her feelings, he would still be hurting her. Being the coward he was, he chose the easy way out. "I just wanted to know that you still like me a little bit. That's all."

She smiled warmly, obviously accepting the opportunity to get out of this uncomfortable conversation as quickly as possible. "You're one of the nicest people I know, Stefan Doffer, and I've seen more than enough wives putting up with husbands who beat them or are always drunk or who keep most of their pay to buy a nice suit for themselves while their children don't have a decent pair of shoes for winter. I'm a lucky woman."

* * * *

Fully satisfied, Stefan retracted his slackened penis from his lover's body and, expecting the same kind of happiness on Adri's face, he smiled. The smile wasn't answered. "Is something wrong? Didn't I leave enough time for you? Was I too rough?"

Adri sighed. "Leave it."

"No, I won't leave it. It's been months since you and I had a chance to share a bed. I was really looking forward to this and it was great, so what's the matter?"

"Yeah, I was looking forward to it too, but what's the use?"

"Sorry, I don't follow you."

"Man and woman complete the puzzle. They form the beginning of a new life. They're what the Bible tells us about. They're natural. What are two men? No history worth telling and no future at all."

Stefan frowned. A cold hand gripped around his heart. "I never thought I'd hear those words from your mouth."

"You have to admit, secret meetings for sex in rented rooms offer a poor alternative to marriage and a family."

"I made our youngest girl because I pestered my wife to allow me. That's how much I wanted you without even having the slightest idea. You made me curious about my own body. You frighten me more than any nightmare and give me more joy that I ever thought possible." To emphasize his words, Stefan kissed his lover. "I have no idea if this thing between us will ever lead to anything at all. All I know is that every day starts with knowing you exist, with knowing how happy I am to see you at our table to share our potatoes and watered-down gravy. I feel miserable and incomplete when I haven't seen you for a week and have no choice but to try and hide the fear that one day it will all be over."

"Is lust enough to fool nature? Is love enough to write history? What if I'm telling myself nothing but fairy tales, and normal people are really right with their instinctive revulsion?"

"Then let them be right. I've heard your pleasure and I'm not blind to the way the expression on your face changes when we meet on the street. Why do you want to break up with me now, after everything we've been through?" Stefan was hardly managing to keep his panic under control. He was finally being given what he had wanted for years, and all he could do was hope that it simply wasn't happening.

Adri shook his head. "I don't want to lose you, not for all the normality and approval in the world. You're my best friend and the only one I've ever wanted with my whole heart and soul, but that doesn't change the facts of my life."

"You're envious because I have a wife and children. Is that it?" guessed Stefan.

"I wish it was that simple, because then I would marry a nice girl and do what's expected of me." Adri paused. "We have nothing tangible to show the world."

Stefan brushed a lock of hair from Adri's forehead, because he couldn't bear not touching him. "Marije never enjoyed the sexual part of our marriage, but she takes her marital duty seriously and so we have two boys and two girls. It is the purpose of marriage, but does it mean more than that there will be a new generation to take care of us when we get old? Some part of you has become part of my family. You watch them grow and none of them remembers there was ever a time without you."

Adri snuggled closer. "We'll never be sure what our love means, but whoever knows a thing like that for sure? People can make children without love, and people can love without making children. I'm here with you because there is no place on this earth I would rather be, and there's no human being, man or woman, in whose arms I'd rather rest. If that's a dead-end street, then so be it."

Stefan placed a finger against Adri's lips to prevent him from speaking any further, and with the other hand, he took the half-empty tin of Vaseline from the bedside table. "It looks like I haven't given you enough this afternoon, so I'll give it another try." He didn't miss the light in his eyes when he scooped up a good dollop of the lubricant.

The sigh of relief from his lover when he entered him once more told him he was doing the right thing.

* * * *

"You won't believe me," said Adri while they were taking their after-dinner walk through the neighborhood, "but today it's exactly six years since we stood in line for that control stamp."

Stefan was honestly surprised. "That long?"

"Well, look at your kids. The eldest is becoming quite a young lady. She's a very clever girl. Pity you and Marije don't have the means to send her to university when she's eighteen."

"Times flies, I know. University is not for our kind, and besides, it would be a waste of money to spend that amount on a girl when she's going to marry and will have to stop working when the first baby arrives. But yeah, she's got a head on her shoulders and I wouldn't be surprised if she ended up marrying a schoolteacher."

Adri hummed his agreement. "She's a born mother. You can already see how much she takes after Marije. The youngest, on the other hand now, is a tomboy if I ever saw one."

"Should I be worried and tell Marije to rein her in a little more?"

"What? A five year old with a bit of spirit? She has two elder brothers. What do you expect?"

"She's different. Sientje is a real girl, the boys are boys, and Ida…"

"Is Ida." Adri touched his hand for a fleeting second while they kept on walking.

"It's getting harder and harder to imagine life without you." Stefan changed the subject back to Adri and himself. "What happened?"

"Nothing more than happens to so many people. You meet someone and you fall in love."

"It's not the same, is it?"

"So what's the difference? I was ill and you took care of me. You're married and I don't want to force you to make an impossible choice. We enjoy each other's company. We long for physical intimacy. What else would you call this but love?" Adri slowed his pace. "That's the problem, isn't it? Love. Lust stops once it's sated, and friendship is innocent enough, but you never know how long love will last. I could leave you and the love might still be there for the rest of your life. You could decide never to see me again, but it might not be enough to stop the love. I love making love with you, but I don't need it to love you—and that is what we couldn't have foreseen, six years ago."

Stefan had no idea what to say in reply to what he knew to be the truth of the matter.

Chapter Seventeen

Stefan had allowed Adri to talk him into visiting the party without really having an idea why. Perhaps the war had changed more than he wanted to admit. A shadow constantly in the background, it somehow wasn't really there, yet still influenced life to the smallest details.

"I know you don't particularly want to know about that part of my life, but please, I'm sure it will be a nice evening. Good people, music and simply being among folks who don't care if a man dances with a man or a woman with a woman. It's being held in a private home, like Jo Swart's, and rich and artistic people go there all the time, so no one will notice."

He said yes, as much to Adri's surprise as his own, but by the time the night of the party arrived, he was too nervous to look forward to it. A promise was a promise, though, and curiosity did the rest. Marije didn't ask about the details, and in return he told as little of a lie as possible.

Adri took him to a house not much smaller than the one he remembered from his visit to Jo Swart, but instead of being detached, it was part of a block of houses.

"Which floor belongs to your friend?"

"All of them, from the basement to the attic. And it's friends, plural, though officially one is a patron for the poor artist and allows him a studio to sleep and work in. Those of us who are in the know, know better," Adri explained casually. He rang the doorbell.

After a short introduction, they were allowed entrance. "Crowded..." Stefan whispered to Adri, who smiled back in reassurance. "And is that a man or a woman?"

"Who knows? Perhaps both?"

The host of the party tapped Adri on his shoulder, nodded at Stefan and asked, "Is this the one?"

"I didn't say a word too much, did I?"

"A redhead... He's gorgeous."

"And mine."

The man grinned. "Lucky bastard."

Stefan didn't feel comfortable to begin with, and all of a sudden he saw something that made him want to leave immediately. "Adri, we can't stay here. There are Krauts here."

Adri put a hand on his arm to calm him down. "Don't panic. Why do you think those men are here? Come on. There's music in the salon and I want to dance."

Both with glasses of wine in their hands, they watched the dancing couples. A woman in suit, her hair short as a man's, led another woman, dressed in a long, elegant gown, to the dance floor. A man with graying hair had his arms around a much younger man.

"Rough trade, if you ask me," Adri explained to Stefan, before he was even able to decide there was anything to ask. "Do you like the wine, by the way?"

Stefan shrugged. "I never drink it, but it's good. I think."

A German officer walked straight across to Adri and invited him for a dance. Adri gestured to Stefan. The officer smiled in understanding, moved his attention to Stefan, made a formal bow and asked, "*Gestatten Sie?*"

Mildly embarrassed by the whole situation, he mumbled to Adri, "You want to dance? Marije tried, when we were engaged, but she gave up after I stepped on her toes one time too many. So if you want to…"

When he saw his lover in the arms of another man, he followed every move with his eyes. The German was attractive enough, with his tall, slim build, dark hair and light blue eyes, and even he could see the man was an excellent dancer. Adri was obviously having a great time.

The upbeat song was being followed by something much slower. "Can I…?" Adri asked and already he and the officer were on the dance floor.

More than once men asked if Stefan would care to dance, but he shook his head absentmindedly. He felt that all his attention must stay focused on Adri, as if even a second of looking away would mean the beginning of disaster. He wasn't blind or stupid. He saw how the German held Adri, how he pulled him just that little bit tighter. His lover looked downright happy, as if he couldn't imagine anything nicer than to slowly dance in the arms of an officer of the German Wehrmacht at an illegal party. He even whispered a few words into the ear of his dancing partner. Stefan's hands shook when he clearly saw how his lover pressed his lips against the officer's neck, even if it was just for a fleeting second. He was jealous enough to feel tears starting in his eyes, and yet he couldn't stop watching the man for whom he was prepared to take any risk. Adri was so unbearably beautiful at that very moment that it broke Stefan's heart.

The German returned Adri to his place, thanked him for the pleasure, said a few words Stefan didn't care to answer, and walked over to the table with the alcoholic drinks. Adri took the glass of wine Stefan was still holding in his hand, emptied it himself and put it down. Then he kissed Stefan full on the mouth.

"There are other people here."

"So?" Adri took him by the hand, leading him out of the salon to a quiet corner near the central stairwell. "You wouldn't have thought it to look at him, but that man was a great dancer."

"I would have given you nothing but bruised toes, so aren't you lucky that a handsome gentleman asked you to dance?" Stefan sneered. "You goddamn kissed him!"

"You call that a kiss? What we do, that's real kissing. But he smelled so nice, and I simply had to give him a little peck." Adri blushed like a schoolboy who had just discovered something new and exciting.

"They reek of leather."

"Boots and belt, at least," Adri sighed happily.

"You're just about ready to drool over that Kraut," exploded Stefan. "I'm beginning to wonder if you wouldn't prefer me to have stayed home with the wife."

"I saw you watching. After all those years I still don't know if I know you all that well, but I do know that look in your eyes when you get really horny. And here you are, talking about me drooling over a handsome man who smells nice." Adri pushed Stefan farther into a corner.

"You were so beautiful and I love you so much. You were so close with that man and you said something to him then you kissed him, and I wanted you so much," Stefan blabbered, while Adri took his face between his hands and covered it with dozens of quick kisses.

"You know what I said to the man I danced with? I said, 'The man who gets you will be one lucky devil, but it won't be me.' A gorgeous man, a good dancer and he smells lovely, but he can't stand in the shadow of my own bloke," Adri whispered, his lips so close to Stefan's ear that the words themselves felt like caresses.

"This isn't the time or the place, because I don't want to embarrass the host or the other guests, but I really need you right now." Stefan had no idea how Adri was able to understand the words whispered against his neck, but his lover took him by the hand and led him up the stairs to the uppermost floor and opened a door to what proved to be a servant's room, although it was obviously no longer in use as such. Below them the noise of music and laughing people continued, but they closed the door behind them and lay down on the narrow bed, both still fully clothed.

Stefan was safe in the arms of his lover, who held him so tightly that it seemed he wanted to destroy the very last physical barrier between them, but Stefan was inconsolable. "I did everything I could to get rid of you, but if you left me, I'd rather die. And even that wouldn't be allowed, because there are people who depend on me. I have nothing interesting to say. I don't feel at ease with your friends and I'm not even really handsome. One day a man is going to smile at you and you'll be his — and if not that, then the Germans will get you."

"I was only flirting. It didn't mean anything. I almost never get the chance to dance with another man. Did it upset you that much?" Adri kissed him. "You turn me on when you get all jealous, do you know that?"

"Did you even listen?"

"I was listening. I just pretended I didn't understand what you were saying." He kissed Stefan again. "I'm going to loosen your clothes — not getting fully naked, mind you — just enough so I'm able to reach what I need to reach then you'll get on your belly and I'm going to fuck you." It was obvious to Stefan his lover was taking full control and he nodded, thankful that for a moment all decisions were out of his hands.

With the help of a small quantity of spit, Adri entered him slowly enough to prevent any real discomfort. Stefan got on his knees and pushed back against him, partly to give him more space to move, but perhaps even more because of the sorrow and grief that washed over him with a fierceness he wasn't prepared for.

"Have you any idea how much I love you? Are you even able to understand it?" Adri grabbed his hips with bruising fingers and started to thrust in and out in a fast, aggressive rhythm. "I love you so much that I wish I had a way to make you hate me, so you could go back to the life you had before you met me."

"Hating you wouldn't change a thing." Stefan groaned when his lover pushed his head against the mattress and forced his legs even wider apart to gain maximum access. "Please, give me everything. Please…"

The pain and the pleasure were so closely connected that they were one and the same. Stefan slumped on the bed, thankful for the arms holding him.

"I'm thirsty." Stefan had to laugh because of the sudden change of mood. "You think they might have left a couple of beers for us? Have you seen the amount of food and drink, by the way?" He pulled up his trousers and sat on the bed again.

Adri leaned on his elbow and yawned. "I'm sure the black market guys did excellent business and the hosts probably had a few good bottles left from before the invasion." He reached for Stefan's right hand and kissed it. "Thanks for allowing me this."

They walked down the stairs to look for beer and something to eat. The officer who had danced with Adri passed them halfway. He greeted them, and Stefan couldn't help but grin triumphantly. He was all too aware that both he and Adri must positively reek of sex. The German seemed to understand and winked at him. Another man, who walked right behind him, placed a hand on his shoulder and the officer smiled fondly.

"On the top floor, at the end of the corridor, there's where you want to be."

With a glass of beer in one hand and nice piece of very mature Gouda cheese in the other they sat on the stairs, watching the comings and goings of the other guests. With some they talked. Others just smiled in understanding.

"I'm so happy," Stefan sighed. "Our country is occupied by Germans, I'm at an illegal party surrounded by people I would have spat at a few years ago and I'm happy."

"Because this is what freedom is all about. Not the stuff that costs money and connections. I mean just us, sitting here. Freedom."

"But isn't it dangerous, parties like this?"

"The Germans hardly care, as long as we keep away from their business. For now, they want the Jews and anyone directly bothering them. Why do you think you see so few German soldiers on the streets? And the ones who are here I personally wouldn't call elite troops." Adri shrugged. "I'm sure it'll be our turn soon enough."

It took Stefan several seconds before he realized that the pounding on the front door meant the end of the party. Then he saw the other guests each react according to their own nature. Some started to run in any direction, while others stood frozen in their conversations.

"Come on. I noticed a hatch in the ceiling of the servant's room. Both at the front door and the garden door there will be police or soldiers, but the roof might give us a chance," Adri explained, taking Stefan by the hand and running with him up the stairs.

Stefan knew this was his punishment. This was how he was going to pay.

Adri kicked open the door of the room where they had shared their pleasure less than half an hour earlier, got the clothes from the floor and threw them on the bed. "Raid," he said simply to the two men, who reacted with shock but remained alert. Then he climbed onto the bed, and for the first time Stefan noticed that Adri was right and there was indeed a hatch in the ceiling.

The naked men hastily dressed and helped Stefan and Adri to climb onto the roof, where they returned the favor. Adri closed the hatch behind the officer's companion. "It gives us a few seconds extra, I hope."

If it had not been for the full moon, the night would have been pitch black in the obligatory blackout. Stefan knew no better than to follow Adri to the edge of the building and accept whatever might happen. They were three floors above street level and to turn back would end, with absolute certainty, in all four of them being arrested.

"We'll have to jump here, but it's not far." Adri pointed into the darkness. "I know a way to get to the street from there. I'll take the first jump, so you can see I'm telling the truth."

Stefan knew this was the exact moment to blindly trust his friend and jump into the night. For a split second he was certain that he'd fall to his death, but then he heard the sound of gravel under his shoes. The officer followed right behind, but the other man seemed to hesitate.

"David, *bitte…*"

But for David, the jump, a distance any healthy man could easily make, proved unbridgeable. "You go on. I'll wait until it gets light."

"Adri? We'd better move on. I'm sorry, but I don't think there's anything we can do right now. If we wait any longer, the Krauts will hear us and we'll all be in trouble."

"David, you don't have to be afraid. You don't even need a run-up. It's really that close," Adri tried.

"*Schon gut.* It's okay. I'll go where you go," the officer said cheerfully. He patted both Stefan and Adri on their shoulders and jumped back across to the house, to whatever destiny awaited him.

Stefan looked back once to the vaguely visible contours of the two men before Adri took his hand and urged him to hurry up. He banned all thought or worry from his head, simply doing what Adri told him to do. He forgot about the people they had left behind, about the risk he had taken and the sheer stupidity of this party even happening and his being there. He just ran and jumped and climbed, and suddenly he found himself with the keys to his own home in his hand, trying to open the door.

He trembled so violently that Adri asked, "Are you okay?"

Stefan shook his head. "No." Too much had happened that night for him to be able to say more. The unusual company, his jealousy, the servant's room, the raid and the narrow escape had all been too much for him to accept so easily that he was safe even now. He was still too confused and scared even to be able to recognize his relief just yet.

Quietly they went inside.

Adri took him into his arms. "I'm so terribly sorry," he said.

"Then don't mention this night ever again."

Chapter Eighteen

For a long time Stefan refused to believe the rumors which now surrounded Jakoba Huyzen. Against his better judgment, he realized, even before he saw the definite proof. She had never been the victim of any gossip, this quiet, unremarkable woman. Even her willingness to order controversial books and pamphlets, something only known in limited circles, hadn't diminished her immaculate reputation. He wished it not to be true, because of her silent understanding of what had happened between him and Adri, and also because she was a friend. Then the talking started, and soon enough Adri told him of several acquaintances who no longer frequented her bookshop. Still, he refused to believe, until one day, when he saw the way a German officer kissed the bookseller, who probably had never been kissed by anyone in all of her forty years.

He told Adri.

"I know about her and Armin. He's an army photographer and a decent bloke—always willing to look the other way, if you know what I mean."

"You personally know that Kraut?" Stefan stared at his lover. Once again he was reminded of the chasm between them, of the life he wasn't part of.

"Let's put it this way. He's good people. Take it from me. There's no reason to doubt Jakoba Huyzen." He discreetly touched Stefan's arm. "This isn't about Jakoba or the fact that she's seeing a much younger German soldier, is it?"

"I... What happened to those men? At that party... Did they get away?"

Adri shook his head. "I'm so sorry."

"It could have been us."

"But it wasn't..."

"No, it wasn't..."

* * * *

Change crept closer to them like a silent killer. Marije, the ever-optimistic one, now openly worried about the unavoidable moment when the food she was able to put on the table would no longer be enough to keep them from going to bed on a half-empty stomach.

"Watery milk, meat you wouldn't give a dog and if the baker dares to tell me his bread is of the same quality as it was before the war, I'll call him a liar right to his face." She looked at her almost empty pantry and sighed. "We'll make do. As long as we have each other, we'll make do. I just wish..."

Stefan didn't know what to say, except platitudes about the Allies building up their armies to crush the Nazis once and for all. He wasn't blind. He saw how poor his family looked, how threadbare their clothes were, how tired and worn-out their faces. But he refused to acknowledge that Adri was becoming more and more withdrawn, guarding secrets that were truly dangerous.

Now and again Adri asked, "Do you mind if I leave this bag here? Someone will collect it tomorrow night." Marije always nodded her consent. Stefan nodded because he had to, and a young woman, Truus or Trees or whatever she was called, would say 'thanks' and a week later Adri would ask again, and Marije said, "Of course, no problem."

Then, one day, the question came, as unexpected as it was unavoidable. "I can no longer stay at my old address…"

"I wish I could do something for you," Stefan said. "But I'll ask around if that helps."

Marije shook her head. "If there's room for your mother, there's room for a friend. He's here often enough to be almost part of the family. You agree with me, *Opoe*?"

Opoe Doffer smiled. "He's a nice young man, but where is he going to sleep?"

"She's right, Marije. Every room in the house, except this one, is crammed with beds already." Stefan tried to be the sensible one. "It's simply impossible."

"Here in the living room, of course. Where else?"

"It's really kind of you," Adri interjected, "but it's too much to ask."

Suddenly Stefan realized something, and he didn't want to share it with either his wife or his mother. He asked Adri to step outside for a moment.

"Why don't you ask one of your friends with big houses and lots of money if they have a spare room?"

Adri looked at him as if he thought his friend was out of his mind. "You're serious? After the way that party ended? I need a safe place, Stefan, not a comfortable one. And I didn't even ask if you'd be willing to risk your family for me, remember?"

"If Marije says there's room for you, then there's room for you. God knows I'm not a hero, but I hope my children will never have to see me refuse a friend a plate of food or a place to sleep. So I guess that pretty much settles it."

"It's too much..."

"It is, and that's still how it's going to happen."

* * * *

The grown-ups counted their blessings. They had each other and a roof over their heads and, despite everything, there was still food on the table. But all the blessings in the world couldn't prevent the countless minor irritations and petty fights. *Opoe* Doffer became even quieter than usual while peeling potatoes. Marije's smile no longer reached her eyes on most days. Stefan fled the house whenever he found an excuse to do so, and Adri hid behind a book.

And still there were nights of quiet contentment, of playing chess, talking about the small events of the day, helping a child with homework. The harmony wouldn't last longer than a few hours, but it was enough to keep life worth living.

Once again, they had brushed against each other while moving through the over-full house. Adri's hand lingered a fraction of a second too long against Stefan's behind.

"I ache so much for you that it makes me desperate," Stefan whispered, "but there's always someone home. I love my mother and I hope she'll be with us for a long time, but we're never alone for even those few hours on Sunday afternoon, because she can't get down the stairs anymore."

"We're going for a walk," Adri decided.

The first smell of autumn hung in the air and with it, the worries about the next winter, but they walked through the streets of the neighborhood with fast, angry paces, not knowing what to do with the surplus of sexual energy.

"I want you like mad. I've almost considered bothering Marije to at least get rid of the itch. I know it won't do me any good and she doesn't deserve to be treated as a dumping-place for my... Well, you know. She'd allow me, as long as the little girl isn't in the same room. She's a good wife who knows her marital duty. But it's you I want." Stefan knew he was feeling sorry for himself, and he wasn't even ashamed about it.

"So, what do we do about it? The urinals? Because the hourly rooms have become too expensive, with the Krauts and all," Adri said with a big grin on his face.

"This isn't funny. We'd get arrested for public indecency before you'd even tasted me, and Marije and my mum would have to worry even more about how they'd manage with the kids and the war!"

They walked home, not knowing where else to go.

"At least we've had a bit of fresh air," Adri said with desperate optimism.

The tension between them crackled with electricity. Without warning, Stefan chased Adri up the stairs, growling at everyone even looking at them. In the boys' bedroom, he barked at the quietly reading Wilfred,

"Get down to your mum and ask if she's got a job for you. If not, you find something. Uncle Adri and I have some talking to do."

All of a sudden, he and Adri were alone in the cramped attic room where a grown man could only stand upright in the exact middle, knowing no one would even dare to come near the door, let alone open it. Stefan loosened his buttons and zipper and dropped his trousers to the floor. "You too." He pulled his lover close and kissed him roughly. He felt no shame at all.

* * * *

Opoe Doffer died as quietly and unobtrusively as she had lived. Death didn't come to her as a sudden, aggressive illness or an accident. The old woman simply faded into the shadows, talking even less than she had in recent months, except for a few words about her late husband. "You remember your dad?"

"Of course I do, Mum. I remember everything."

"I miss him." She looked so small and insignificant in the chair Stefan had made for his bride, and yet she was the center of the room, of the family. She no longer saw much of the others through the mist of her cataracts, but Stefan knew even Ida looked often at her *Opoe*, making sure she would still be there for another day.

On the night that was to be her last, Stefan and Adri helped her to her bed. She leaned so fully on them that they were practically carrying her. His mother had become so light that Stefan couldn't imagine how she had ever carried him in her arms for hours. Carefully the men put her on the bed and waited while Marije helped her to change into her nightgown.

Adri must have seen his sad eyes, because he put a hand on his shoulder and pulled him close for a second. He didn't protest the all-too-public show of affection.

"Sleep well, boys," she said when Stefan and Adri left the room so Marije could do her work.

"She always says that, 'Sleep well, boys'," Stefan said, though he had no idea why he suddenly noticed it.

The next morning Sientje, her face white with worry, screamed that *Opoe* didn't answer her when she said good morning. "Is she sick, Mum? She can't be mad at me, can she? I was extra careful not to make a noise when I needed to use the night pot."

A single look was enough for Stefan to be certain that his mother had died.

* * * *

For weeks Stefan more than once saw Marije crying into her apron, but he no longer knew how to take her in his arms to console her. He felt helpless to tell her how much he missed the old woman, but also how much he worried about Adri during the hours when he left the house without ever saying where he was going and why. He worked, was a father to his children, did whatever jobs needed to be done around the house and still he was a stranger in his own home. When Adri asked the question he had already been expecting, he wasn't the one to make the final decision but Marije — and it was Marije who went with Trees or Truus, to come back with a tiny bundle in her arms. He set up the cradle in a corner of their bedroom, knowing this baby would be the first of many.

Young women he hardly knew the first name of brought packages and infants. Other young women, equally strangers to him, would collect them a day later. Marije never refused and he didn't say a thing. His veto would have been ignored.

The first Sunday Marije went to visit family, taking the children with her, he landed on the bed with Adri and they made love exactly as he expected it to happen, but it wasn't what he had hoped for.

"Is something wrong?" asked Adri. "You've had your pleasure, but please don't tell me it gave you much joy."

"I know you're not telling me exactly what you're doing, but I want to know your reasons. If something bad happens to you, I need to know why. Will it be worth my tears when the Germans finally get you?"

Adri kissed him. "It just happened. I'm not even sure how. An acquaintance of an acquaintance asked for a small favor. Marije and you have your little guests from time to time, a suitcase you never open, both being collected in the morning. Don't you?"

"You expected us to refuse? You know how it is with Marije and babies. That has nothing to do with being part of the Resistance."

Adri shook his head. "That is exactly what it's about, Stefan. Hiding a child so it can be saved for its family, its people, goes right against whatever the Nazis are planning for that child. So does spreading news that's actual news and not propaganda, and doing whatever needs to be done to let those German bastards know that not all of us signed the capitulation. It can't stay the way it is, you know, or even get back to the way it was before."

"What do you mean by that?" It bothered Stefan that he no longer understood his friend. "You mean everything will change after the war?"

"Of course. Once they hear how many perverts and degenerates and inverts made and spread illegal newspapers, forged IDs and coupons for food and clothing, found the money to pay for it all, opened their houses to Jews and illegal workers in danger of getting arrested, sabotaged German military targets... The normal people will look at us with changed eyes."

"Why do you sound as if you don't believe your own words?"

"Because I know too damn well that what people want when this is all over is everything going back to normal. They want young married couples and lots of babies. People don't want different. They want what they know." Adri sounded almost fatalistic.

"You think everything will be exactly like before? Isn't that a bit too pessimistic?"

"Be honest. What do you want, once the Allies have kicked the Germans home?"

"That everything will be like it used to be, with Marije and the children. With you. You'll eat supper with us. We'll take a walk through the neighborhood, and now and again we'll rent a room..." Stefan stopped talking because slowly he realized what he was saying.

"They'll forget about us, Stefan—or, more likely, they'll never acknowledge guys like us risked our necks for a society that prefers not to know we even exist."

"I don't know what to say." Stefan knew few people who were more courageous and honest than Adri, but he had as much illusion about everyday reality as his friend. The opportunities to behave like lovers, instead of just good friends, were extremely limited—to put it mildly—because every touch, kiss, word or even the wrong look outside the strict privacy of a locked room could get them into deep trouble.

"Why don't you just tell me I should stop with my self-pity?" Adri kissed Stefan's cheek. "In the end it's all pretty simple, isn't it? Those German soldier boys in the school next to Huyzen's bookshop might all be decent individuals in their heart of hearts, and a few of them are handsome enough, but I don't want to see them marching through our streets in uniform pretending to be in charge. And yeah, perhaps my love for you gives me strength to continue when I'm scared. So what? I'm only human."

"I remember the political discussions you tried to start before the war. We even had a fight about it, because I couldn't care less. You were right, though."

"Everything I do, every step, I make sure you're there too. I've made peace with the knowledge that what I do may land me in prison, or worse, but I have a much harder time accepting that I put you and your family in any danger. I know that resistance against the Germans is impossible if I want to live according to the rules my mother taught me. You know them too, the ones about speaking the truth, not stealing, respect for your betters... I learned to lie, steal and endanger the lives of others who don't even know half of what I'm doing. The end might justify the means, but no one's going to tell me I'll ever get my hands clean again." Adri kissed his lover. "Don't worry. It went the way it had to go and whatever happens is, for the most part, out of our hands. You don't ask, so I don't have to answer you."

"It's time to get up and straighten the bed." Stefan hid his concern behind a harsh voice. He almost regretted not having joined Marije and the children on their family visit. He regretted ever having asked questions he didn't want the answers to.

Chapter Nineteen

"Shall we go inside for a cup of coffee?" Adri suggested. "It looks like a nice place. My treat."

Stefan wasn't so sure about it. "There might be Krauts too."

"So? They're everywhere. Please, indulge me?" Adri tried to persuade him. "I just want to drink a cup of coffee with you in a restaurant. Like a normal couple."

The establishment was clean and cozy in a reassuring manner, with nothing to intimidate a respectable working-class family. It was quite full but they found a place at the window. "That way we can see who passes by."

The ersatz was acceptable enough, and they drank it as slowly as possible. Even though they behaved in an inconspicuous manner, the simple pleasure of sitting at the table in a public place, drinking coffee, was a rare and festive occasion. They watched people going by— a housewife with a wicker grocery basket in one hand and a sniveling toddler in the other one, a baker's helper on a delivery bicycle, an old man wearing a black suit with a mourning band around his right arm, an NSB man in uniform.

"Seeing a handsome man?" Adri asked *sotto voce*.

Stefan was startled.

"Well?"

"You're sitting here right before me. Why would I be looking at other men? Are you?" Stefan wasn't sure his voice didn't sound a little bit jealous.

"Across the street, at the newspaper stand. Look there." Adri nodded his head in a particular direction.

"I see no one except a couple of Germans."

"Look closer."

"Look closer at what, the usual bloody uniforms?"

"There's something between those two."

"I don't get you. What is supposed to be going on between them?"

"Exactly what's going on between us."

"You mean...?"

"They're a couple, or else there's something seriously wrong with my eyes."

"Well, there must be something wrong with mine. I don't see anything."

"Pay attention. They're standing just a fraction too close together, but not so close that others would notice, and one is touching the other ever so slightly. See how they look at each other then look away?"

Stefan shook his head. "I'm sorry. There are two Wehrmacht soldiers being terribly bored, and that's it."

"You're probably right about them being bored, because they're coming this way. By the way, did you honestly not notice that one of them isn't exactly ugly?"

The door of the restaurant opened and, in spite of himself, Stefan looked over his shoulder. "I'm married.

Why would I look at other men? But I admit I've seen uglier Krauts."

"Nice try, but even the biggest lady-killer will turn his head when that man walks by. Have the honesty to recognize beauty when you see it, Stefan."

Only then Stefan did notice that all tables in the restaurant were at least partly occupied. He looked straight ahead when the soldier asked if the remaining two chairs at their table were free but Adri nodded, grinning at his friend. "Let's see what happens."

The soldiers ordered their coffee. They talked to each other in quiet voices and didn't seem too interested in the men next to them. Beneath their uniforms most likely they were regular men, and yet there was something that made Stefan doubt his own observation. Within a quarter of an hour, the table would be empty again and he still wouldn't know if Adri had been pulling his leg about the soldiers being a pair.

Almost by accident he caught the look in the eyes of the soldier sitting next to Adri and he knew what they both were seeing, that stranger and he. They both reached for their cigarettes to deal with the awkwardness of the moment.

"*B-b-b-bitte, n–n-ni-mmen Sie*," the man offered, his brow furrowed in concentration.

An ordinary bloke, Stefan thought, never noticed by anyone. Until someone with devilish lights in his eyes came along and nothing would ever be the same again. He accepted the cigarette, because it was the only way to let the man know he recognized and understood.

Adri and the other man were having a conversation in a mixture of German and Dutch. Quiet country, people were relatively easy to deal with, nothing much happening. No, they weren't complaining. They had lodgings in the school across from that bookshop. Were the Dutchmen familiar with it?

In all those years since Adri had first kissed him at the stairwell, Stefan had rarely been in the company of those who felt the way he did and never with anyone that he was almost able to identify with. It made him uncomfortable, but it also made him want to stay, because, no matter how deep his aversion, the need to look beyond the loneliness of his existence was stronger than all other emotions, if only for a moment.

"Stefan, we have to go." Adri quickly touched his hand, as a last confirmation of what must have been clear from the beginning.

Stefan forced himself not to look back. Nothing had happened, and nothing ever would.

"Shall we walk to the park? They said they'll be going there too." Adri sounded in a particularly good mood.

Stefan had to make sure he understood what he was hearing. "They?"

"Those Germans, of course. We can't really talk in that restaurant, can we?"

"And you decided that all by yourself, without asking my opinion? Well, thank you very much. That's just what we need — being seen with a couple of Krauts by half the town!"

"You're free to go home. I won't blame you. I don't have a family, after all. I'll tell you all about it, okay?" Adri stayed eerily cheerful.

"You don't seriously think I'd leave you alone with those Krauts, do you?" Stefan became serious angry about the suggestion alone. "What do they want from us, anyway?"

"The same thing we want from them?"

"They're still Krauts."

"And they run the same risk as us of getting arrested. They're just as surprised to meet people they have this in common with. That's why I see my friends at Jo's and read those books and pamphlets. No one wants to be alone and isolated, Stefan, no one."

In the quietest corner of the town's park they waited until, much to Stefan's surprise, the two German soldiers walked in their direction. Two men in Feldgrau, risking everything to say the unspeakable words, to give what was necessarily hidden its place in the sun.

The dark-eyed soldier with a smile to melt iron introduced himself and his companion. "This here is Achim Händler and I'm Christoph von Fernhauser."

"Stefan Doffer and Adri Heyman," Adri said. "I saw you at the other side of the street. I noticed something about the two of you right away. You couldn't see us in that restaurant, could you?"

"We just felt like a cup of coffee and to sit down for a bit."

"You speak Dutch pretty fluently. How come?"

"I spent my holidays here when I was a boy, because one of my grandparents had Dutch friends. And we've been here for a while now."

"You can say that again." Stefan couldn't stop himself. He noticed that the soldier called Achim understood enough of his words to feel embarrassed by them.

"We're not going to win this war," Christoph admitted cheerfully. "Not in the long run."

"Not an opinion you should share with anyone," Stefan warned. "Not all Dutch are to be trusted, I'm ashamed to say."

"You two are." Christoph looked him straight in the eye.

Stefan shrugged. "That depends on who you're asking."

"So you walked into that restaurant and looked for a table to sit down." Adri restarted the story.

"I noticed a table by the window with two gentlemen," Christoph continued.

"There were several attractive-looking young ladies, if I'm not mistaken. And what if we had been waiting for female company?"

"Were you?" Christoph smiled knowingly.

"I'm married. My wife and I have two boys and two girls," Stefan said, more out of habit than to actually prove anything.

"You're not the only one." Christoph didn't seem impressed by the announcement. "I saw how you looked at each other."

"We try to be discreet." Stefan worried about the other man's words. If it was so obvious to total strangers, how much longer could he and Adri remain safe in anonymity?

"You can only see what you're able to see," Adri explained. "Outsiders will always see us as normal because we look it and we behave normally. They can't even imagine anything else."

"He's right, although you still have to be careful these days," Christoph admitted.

"How bad is it, actually? I've heard the rumors, but..." Stefan asked without really wanting to hear the answer.

"They're not interested in immoral behavior among citizens. They assume the Dutch authorities will take care of that, as long as there are no German soldiers involved."

"So that pretty much means the same misery as before."

"Wehrmacht soldiers can expect prison, with suicide battalion as a non-optional extra — and if you're SS, you should be very certain that the sex will be good enough to die for. Individual variations not included."

Stefan couldn't believe the indifference in Christoph's voice. "You sound as if you don't care. Aren't you afraid?"

"If you never truly lived and loved, what have you lived for anyway? And we all die, one way or the other. I'm not suicidal, so I'm careful, but I don't want to die inside a little more with each new day because I have to hide my love for Achim, even for his own sake." Christoph smiled at his lover. "He makes it all worthwhile."

Achim visibly didn't know where to look.

"But how have you managed to keep it hidden from the rest of your company?" Stefan remembered the mobilization. Except for that one meeting in a hotel, he and Adri hadn't had a single chance to meet in private.

"Be damned careful, and be very lucky with your comrades, because there's plenty of people more than happy to betray their mates for having a bit of fun." Christoph no longer smiled. "Makes you wonder what they have to hide."

"You two obviously made it this far."

"If you pay attention, you'll still sometimes find a *mensch*, a decent human being, in Germany."

"Have you two been together all that time?" Stefan wanted to know, though he knew it was none of his business.

"Since we were recruits, back in '39." Christoph looked at Achim for a second or two. "He attracted attention by his total lack of talent for all things military. It's a miracle the drill sergeant didn't kill him out of pure desperation. During the assault course, he fell flat on his face, right at my feet, and from that day to this, I can't imagine life without him."

"It was 1935 and we were standing in line to get the control stamp for welfare. I saw the redhead in front of me, and that was that." Stefan heard Adri say the familiar words. Their secret had been shared with strangers, but he understood why it had to happen in the name of fairness.

"I can imagine it. Redheads..." Christoph grinned at Adri, and Stefan noticed a happy understanding between the two men. He didn't want any man to look at his friend that way, even if it was a man he could hardly keep himself from blatantly staring at. Achim he had recognized in an instant, as if they were kin, but Christoph scared him because of the gulf between loving one special, individual man and suddenly realizing he was able to feel physically attracted to a man who wasn't Adri.

"I have to go home. Marije will be waiting."

They said their goodbyes, made vague promises to meet again and went their own way.

"Decent guys." Adri looked at the soldiers walking away from them.

Stefan nodded absentmindedly, deep in thought about what had happened that afternoon.

"Let me be absolutely clear about one thing. You belong to me and I belong to you. On that condition, I'm okay with it, redhead."

Stefan's heart skipped a beat. "What are you talking about?" As if he didn't know.

"You have my full and heartfelt permission."

Stefan frowned, because if this was a joke, he wasn't sure he liked it. Adri was giving him something he hadn't asked for and didn't need. Was this his way of telling him that everything had its natural ending?

* * * *

Christoph showed them a holiday home a full hour's bike ride from the city. "I spent a few summers here as a boy, with friends of my grandmother's family. My parents had already died by that time," he said. "I learned to swim here, and to ride a bike and kiss. In that order, yes."

The house looked as if no family had spent their vacation in it for a long time, but Adri looked around and nodded approvingly. "Lots of space and privacy."

"I remembered it and went looking. It was easy to get in," Christoph said.

Stefan didn't trust what he was being told. "You don't know where those friends are now?"

"In fact I do, somewhere in England. Last time I heard from them, they were living with family until they could afford their own place. They got out in time. It was good to hear that. They won't mind if I invite a few friends." Christoph pulled up a chair and sat down. He looked totally at ease, and Stefan had no difficulty believing he would probably feel at ease in any situation—as if Christoph couldn't even imagine anyone who wouldn't welcome his company. He wasn't blinkered or vain, Stefan thought. He simply hadn't met with a refusal from anyone. And, he had to admit, it was nearly impossible to stay angry in the face of such a captivating smile. Christoph's trusting nature, bordering on naivety, was perhaps his only true protection against the danger threatening him and his lover. His almost blatant visibility made him invisible to the unbelieving eye.

Achim, the silent one who never seemed to be more than two steps away from Christoph, walked to the door. Adri followed him, as if they had an agreement they had forgotten to tell Stefan about. Both men looked over their shoulders at the same time and smiled. Stefan didn't understand why he was letting them go.

"You know when I was absolutely certain about the two of you?" Christoph asked. "When I saw the way Adri looked at you. You are a lucky man, Stefan, and I know about luck."

Stefan nodded. "I would have grown old, quietly and happily, if he'd never noticed me."

"How could anyone not notice you?" Christoph lit up a cigarette, plucked it from his mouth and gave it to Stefan.

"The same as Adri..." The intimacy of the gesture shocked Stefan.

"I'm not even sure when it started, but Achim and I always clean each other's rifles and boots. As long as those things are okay, nothing bad will ever happen to us," offered Christoph in return.

"The rest doesn't matter. As long as your weapon and your boots are in working order, you've got a chance in any war." Stefan understood the ritual.

"I've never, and I do mean *never*, been in a foxhole without him, and even if the sky comes down on our heads, we always end up at the same spot. It would be a clever man who saw the chance to shoot one of us without the other. Not going to happen," Christoph said calmly.

Stefan took a long draw from his cigarette. What could he place against this declaration of absolute love? Adri lived in the center of his soul, but his family made it impossible for him to rule sovereign over his own life.

Christoph stood up, took what remained of Stefan's cigarette, stubbed it together with his own and led him to the bedroom where the beds, covered with gray blankets, were waiting for the owners' holiday.

I have never done this before and never even contemplated doing it, Stefan wanted to say. *My marital bed I share with my wife, and my body with the man I love with all my heart and soul. Yet I'm here, with you, a stranger, an enemy, with whom I'm not even in love.*

But he didn't say any of those words because Christoph started to kiss him, simply demanding all his attention. So yes, kissing an unbelievably attractive stranger wasn't quite the same thing as kissing his lover of several years, but the man was a great kisser.

"You're thinking too much." Christoph chuckled, starting to unbutton his uniform jacket. "This is a purely physical experience for both of us, so why are you pretending it isn't happening to your body?"

"It's not that easy," Stefan tried.

"It's the easiest thing in the world. We're two men. We get naked and we have sex."

"We could die because of it."

"It's war. We could die for any number of reasons."

They lay naked on the gray blanket. For the first time Stefan looked at the body of another man, a man who wasn't his lover. He touched the skin with the tips of his fingers, for now more with curiosity than lust.

Christoph was more slenderly muscled, had less body hair and longer limbs than Adri.

Christoph smiled. "How's the other body?"

"A body. We all have them." The truth behind the gruff words was that Stefan was fascinated, enthralled even. Adri's body was deeply loved because of what Adri was to him, but Christoph's was an object of male beauty for the sake of beauty. He wanted to take possession of it, if only once. Nevertheless his hand shook slightly when he wrapped his fingers around the shaft of Christoph's erection. Of course it was as warm as Adri's, but what had he expected? He pumped a few times up and down until a drop of pre-cum formed on the head that he swiped up with his thumb and brought to his mouth. The taste was good enough for Stefan to consider sucking him off, but there was something he wanted even more.

Christoph grabbed his uniform jacket and searched through one of the pockets. He held up a small tin of Vaseline. "You might need this."

"Oh… You expected to—"

"What do you think would have happened between Achim and me if you and Adri hadn't shown up?" Christoph chuckled. "What do you think is going to happen after you and Adri have left?"

"So what do you need me for?"

"The same thing you need me for." Christoph kissed Stefan before he took his hand and guided it to his backside. "To fuck."

"We both already have someone to do that with."

"Ah, but I need to go away sometimes to remind me of where I belong, and you have a question that needs to be answered. Adri has been your first and only one so far, hasn't he?"

Without saying another word Stefan took the tin of Vaseline, gestured Christoph to open his legs and used a good dollop to open him up. Only when Christoph indicated he was ready to get on all fours did Stefan stop him with a short, "I want to see your face, so I know you're not him."

"You're not really worried about that," Christoph stated while he touched Stefan's erection.

Stefan shrugged. "Perhaps not. Are you ready?"

He slowly pushed in, not familiar with Christoph's body and remembering all too well the discomfort of his own first time, but then he remembered the man was anything but a beginner, and looking at his face he saw a smile of welcoming delight.

He was too excited and too nervous to make it last, but he was almost proud to see Christoph reaching his climax right before his own body shuddered in deep pleasure.

Christoph took him in his arms and kissed him. "Thank you."

Stefan laced his shoes and walked outside to see where Adri and Achim were. He had to tell his lover what had happened.

* * * *

"Well?" Adri asked, as soon as they were alone again.

"Well what?" Stefan pretended not to understand.

"How was it? How was he?" Adri beamed, as if he had given Stefan a special birthday present and wanted to know if his friend was honestly happy about it.

"Who says something happened between us?" Stefan didn't understand why he was even trying to pretend. Adri had all but pushed him in Christoph's direction, even though he still didn't understand what he expected to get out of the arrangement. "I'm sure you can guess what happened."

"Of course I know what happened."

"Why did you leave me alone with that German?"

"He would never take you away from me. And I knew that once your curiosity had been satisfied — about whether you could be attracted to any other man enough to have sex with him — you'd come back to me. Consider it a special treat. How could this possibly be a threat to us, when even your sense of duty toward your family couldn't tear us apart?" If Adri felt any jealousy, he certainly managed to hide it perfectly. "Consider what happened today a small miracle."

"I fucked a man I don't even love. Where do you see the miracle?" Stefan would rather deal with cold envy than this smiling approval. After years of cheating on his wife, he had also cheated on his lover. He should have been stronger, resisted temptation.

"You're still expecting punishment, aren't you? But you're already punishing yourself — and you have been, for as long as I can remember. And, by the way, when two strangers — enemies even — meet and take a risk that could threaten their lives, and they trust the other enough to show what everyone considers unspeakable, then yes, I call that a miracle."

"I expected you to say that it's not every day a dime-a-dozen family man of way over thirty ends up in bed with a young man of exceptional beauty," Stefan sneered.

Adri frowned. "Thanks for implying I have bad taste in men. Have you actually looked at Christoph's lover? A stuttering dud, if you insist on being brutally honest about it. And did you happen to notice that Mr.

Looking-like-an-angel worships the stuttering dud to the point that he's actually willing to die for him?"

"We had sex on that bed, but we both knew the truth," Stefan was finally ready to admit what had happened. "He would never make love with anyone but Achim, and I would never make love with anyone but you."

"We walked around, Achim and I. He doesn't speak enough Dutch, nor I enough German, to have a real conversation, but we still got the message across quite well."

"You and he... You didn't...?"

"Not even a kiss. Don't get me wrong, he's a nice bloke and attractive enough if you take the trouble of actually looking at him, but why do you think we stepped outside instead of going to the other bedroom? And no, that's not a question."

"Let the angel and the redhead have their fun?"

Adri chuckled. "That sounds like a novel I would love to read."

Chapter Twenty

Marije put on her coat. "You'll have to look after the kids for a few hours because I'm needed at Jakoba's."

"Why does it have to be you?" It must have been the first time Stefan had seriously contemplated forbidding his wife to do anything. "What will the neighbors say?"

"Not much that's good, I assume. But she's without family or female friends who know about becoming a mother the first time, and she's ill. There's bread, some potatoes and hopefully Adri will bring something later today. I've sent Sientje to the greengrocer's because they said there would be carrots and onions without coupons. The boys and Ida are playing outside, but I warned them to get home in time. Did I forget anything?" She kissed Stefan on the cheek and was gone before he could even say she was right.

Of course she was right, even though she didn't fully appreciate how right, because he himself didn't know all the dangerous truth, but it was enough to face the gossiping neighbors.

As soon as Adri arrived, he told him what was going on and his friend nodded in agreement. "She doesn't deserve to be treated like a traitor. All those good little citizens with their small minds won't believe their ears and eyes when they find out the truth about Jakoba Huyzen after the liberation."

"Of which you know more than just about anyone."

Silently Adri caressed Stefan's hand.

That afternoon they cooked supper, much to the amusement of the children. "Dad is pretending to be Mum, and Uncle Adri is too. That's so funny." Wilfred couldn't stop laughing.

"Eat your potatoes and carrots and don't dare to say this isn't the best, most delicious dinner you've ever had," Adri said with an almost-straight face. "Your daddy and I are the best cooks in the whole world. What am I saying? In the whole universe!"

"Not true," Ida said, biting into an undercooked carrot. "Mum is the best."

"Except for your mum, of course," he admitted with a big smile.

Stefan preferred not to speak his mind about the sobering fact that food had been so scarce for months now that everything that Marije put in front of the children was eaten with the same enthusiasm. Their mother making a white-bread sandwich with strawberry jam for a fussy eater? When was the last time that had happened? And of course you can't have an extra potato, so thanks, children, for not asking.

After she had done the dishes, Sientje played chess with her uncle, the boys did their sums for school and Ida made a drawing of what Stefan thought looked like an English fighter plane hunting a German soldier. He quietly observed his lover and was so happy at this moment of peace that he had to look away to be able to take the next breath.

The sound of the front door being opened startled him. He helped the children to bed, Marije made fresh surrogate coffee and Adri rolled two cigarettes that didn't contain even a gram of real tobacco.

Marije sat down to tell them how Jakoba was doing. "She has a high fever and the baby is very small, but when I left for home, they were both still alive. They should go to hospital, of course, but nowadays staying where they are might be for the best. At least there's one thing that poor little creature has going for her with a German army photographer for a daddy — Armin knows how to find good food for her mum and fuel to keep the room warm." She sighed. "Jakoba can't nurse the little girl because of a serious infection. Cow milk is too rich for a premature baby and there won't be a young mother in this town willing to wet-nurse the child of a Dutch woman and a German soldier living out of wedlock."

"Miserable situation," Stefan acknowledged.

"The last few people who still feel a thread of friendship for that poor woman have promised to visit regularly. I'll go once a day to help with the baby, change the bed, do some laundry. I'll see if there are still any usable clothes from when Ida was a baby, though we gave away most of it to our little guests a few months ago. She has so little for a newborn in the house. It's almost as if she didn't wanted to admit that a child was on its way."

"And the shop?" Adri asked.

Marije frowned. "Are there still any customers left, except for the Germans in the school? And does the shop even matter right now?"

"You're right," admitted Adri, "renting books is not important at the moment." But Stefan could tell from his face that the closing of the bookshop would make for some serious trouble and complications.

* * * *

Marije had to remind them several times before Stefan and Adri summoned up their courage and went to the house of the bookseller. "And I've knitted some socks from a jumper Ida has really outgrown now. It's blue wool, not really suitable for a baby girl, but we all have to make do these days, and it's complicated enough to keep your family warm and fed."

Stefan walked next to Adri through the silent streets of their town. A fine rain drizzled down on them. "You remember…?"

"I touched you between the bookcases. I teased you and you were so shy about it. In hindsight it was all so innocent." Adri bumped against him. "Sorry."

"You did that on purpose."

"Yeah, I did."

The moment they walked into the bedroom, they knew Marije hadn't exaggerated in what she had told them about the condition of the new mother. Jakoba, even in her best years a thin woman without much in the way of female curves, was now skeletal and as pale as death, taking up next to no space in the bed. She opened her eyes when Armin said there were visitors and she smiled in recognition. With a tenderness that made Stefan feel like an intruder, the photographer caressed her hands, asking whether she needed anything.

"Take a seat. I'll make coffee." Armin invited him and Adri to the living room. Not even he had real coffee, but there was some sugar and that was luxury in itself.

"How are you holding out at the moment?" Adri asked him the only question that mattered.

"Yesterday the fever went down for the first time. She's not out of the woods yet, but I'll take care of her the best I can. I know she'll recover," Armin said cheerfully, as if unwilling to see how ill Jakoba actually was. "I have some money and things to trade, so I can get everything she and the baby need. Friends help. Marije's teaching me how to take care of the little girl."

A small cry sounded, making him stand up immediately to go to a corner of the room where the cradle was hidden behind a screen. "To keep everything quiet around her, and to have her close enough to hear when she needs me," he explained, taking the tiny bundle into his hands. With more aptitude than Stefan would expect in any man, the new father attempted to deduce what could be the matter.

Armin talked to his daughter in a soothing voice while he heated up a baby bottle with milk, made sure it was at just the perfect temperature, then sat down with her. Patiently he waited until she had finished drinking, after which he held her in an upright position close to his body, her head hidden against his shoulder. Her tiny body relaxed visibly.

"I never dared to dream Koba would make me a father, but it hurts to see her this ill," Armin said.

"And the little one, she's healthy?" Stefan asked, because as a father he was almost able to forget the other man was a propaganda officer of the enemy and for a moment he felt Armin's worries as his own.

"She's very tiny, but strong. I keep her warm and give her milk every time she asks for it. When she's lonely, she sleeps in my arms. I don't want her to cry. The midwife said I should keep her home, take care of her. Friends bring me a can of goat's milk every day. She's small, but healthy," Armin struggled to find exactly the right words. His Dutch was excellent, but heavily accented.

Stefan didn't think he had ever seen a smaller baby. Even Sientje, who had looked like a tiny doll when he had held her in his arms for the first time, had been a round and robust baby in hindsight. Armin had little chance in this battle. Marije helped day after day in a house where a new life had been welcomed, but where death had entered right after the midwife and was still waiting patiently in the corner of the room.

He wanted to stand up from his chair and leave this dreadful, lonely place. He looked at Adri, who smiled ruefully.

"We won't take more of your time, but if there's anything we can do... Marije will be here tomorrow." As Stefan talked, the doorbell jingled.

"I'll see who's there," Adri offered.

"*Mensch*, Stefan..." Christoph greeted him with a wide grin and an outstretched hand. For a second something fluttered inside his stomach when he felt the hand in his.

Achim nodded his greeting, mumbled something in German and walked to the bedroom to see Jakoba.

If Armin wondered how the men had met, he didn't show it. He simply put the baby carefully back in her crib, made fresh coffee and asked Stefan and Adri to stay a bit longer.

"We got something for you," Christoph said and he brought out a parcel packed in brown paper. "There's real coffee, tea, honey, a bottle of red wine and a chicken. And if you don't ask us where we found this, I won't have to lie to you."

"As long as it helps Jakoba, I'm not asking questions," Armin chuckled.

They were the most unlikely company in an unlikely time, each of them vulnerable to the monsters that lurked outside, but they turned their backs to it and drank coffee in honor of the new father and his daughter.

Chapter Twenty-One

Not since the time of Adri's illness several years ago had Stefan seen his lover looking as pale as he did when he sat down to drink the ersatz coffee Marije had made for him.

"Is everything okay?" she asked him.

Adri shrugged. "It's not important."

Marije didn't ask any further.

"I think we need to talk in private. We're going for a walk," Stefan decided as soon as they finished their coffee. He shoved his slowly reacting friend out of the room. "Don't worry about it, girl. We'll be back in time for supper."

Without saying a word they walked to the park to sit on the familiar bench. Stefan looked out of the corners of his eyes at the man plucking nervously at his already threadbare trousers. "You're shivering. I wish I could take you in my arms."

"I wish you could do that, yes." Adri managed a smile, but it didn't speak of much joy. "They've arrested him."

Instinctively Stefan knew right away who Adri meant. "You were there when they arrested Jo? Did the Krauts see you? Are you in any danger?"

"Is that all you're worried about? Me? The man who took care of me when I had no one and nothing is in German hands! Did you hear what I said? They have Jo Swart!" Adri spit out his angry words. "And you're worried about me?"

"I'm worried about you, yes. I'm your friend or have you forgotten that? I like to pretend I'm perhaps more than a friend. So, does he know what you're doing? You understand what I mean, don't you?" Stefan lighted a cigarette. He didn't enjoy it, but Marije had given up part of her sugar ration for a carton of cigarettes and so he kept on smoking.

"I promised him never to talk about it with anyone outside our circle. He hasn't been arrested because of what he does for the underground, and I doubt they'll even ask him about it. I'll make myself invisible for a while, but I don't expect any problems. I'm sick with worry about Jo, though. What will happen to him?" Adri accepted a puff from Stefan's cigarette.

"What exactly did he do?" Stefan asked, though he wasn't sure if he was ready for the answer.

"An acquaintance, someone I met a couple of times at Jo's, told me he'd been caught in a public urinal. A middle-aged gentleman, who always stayed far from such places." Adri shook his head. "I still can't believe it. I understand that some men are desperate, but Jo's always been set on good manners and showing that men like us can be exactly as morally principled as normal people."

"But the Krauts don't bother with his—our—kind, or did I misunderstand Christoph? So he's arrested by our police, he gets a few months of prison—or perhaps even only a fine since he has the money for a lawyer—and that's it." Stefan tried to make it sound reasonable.

"He was caught in the act of sucking off an SS-man."

Stefan gasped for air.

"I don't think I've ever met anyone with higher morals, and now he does a thing like this! He didn't even take the man to a discreet location. It happened in a urinal, with an SS-man in uniform. They must have been suicidal, both of them." Adri was obviously having trouble believing his own words.

"You're not planning on doing anything to get him out of jail, I hope?"

"I'm not that crazy. This has nothing to do with the Resistance. If he's allowed to correspond with friends or family, I'll try to make sure he gets whatever he needs, but that's all I can do." Adri turned to Stefan. "I'm afraid I'll never see him again."

"Come home with me. It's time for supper," was the only thing Stefan could think of saying.

* * * *

"I have to get out of town for a while, Stefan. As soon as I have a safe address, I'll let you know so you can visit me." Adri said this bluntly, right after Marije had gone upstairs to tell the boys it was time to go to sleep.

"Are the Krauts looking for you after all? Has it anything to do with Jo Swart?"

"I would have been picked up already had that been the case. The less you know, the better."

Stefan was baffled at how calm and almost indifferent his lover sounded. "You're in danger and you're shutting me out."

"I'm a single man. You have a wife and four children."

It was all very reasonable, but Stefan didn't want to hear about reason. "You've got me—but that doesn't count, does it?"

Adri gently put a hand on Stefan's arm. "I don't want to be away from you, not even for a week, but I'd rather leave you and return than stay to get arrested and probably end up in some concentration camp in Germany, because then I'd never see you again."

"But please come back to me."

* * * *

Adri's shirt, worn only a day ago, lay forgotten on the bed. Stefan took it in his hands and brought it close to his face. The scent of his lover was still there. He opened his mouth, wanted to stuff the fabric in. He was suffocating in uncertainty and he had no one to talk about the fear he kept hidden deep inside.

For a moment, he considered putting on the shirt as an impotent protection against the pain that clawed his guts into shreds until he had puked out everything in his stomach.

Instead, he crumpled the shirt and threw it into the washtub.

* * * *

Adri was in danger. Adri had forgotten about him. Why didn't he send Trees or Truus to tell him, 'A certain individual we both might know asked me to tell you that everything is okay.' Didn't he understand that four weeks without news was enough to drive Stefan up the wall? One couldn't be careful enough, with the Krauts and traitors hunting for him, but this was positively inhuman.

"Stefan, I almost forgot to tell you, but there was a young lady at the door to give you a letter. You weren't here, so..."

He all but tore the paper from his wife's hand, read the address and knew everything was going to be fine.

"Adri is safe."

"Perfect, then you can take him his clean laundry." Marije smiled when he kissed her. "My, that's been a while."

* * * *

The farmer's wife welcomed him with a friendly nod. "You're Adri's friend? Stefan Doffer? Red hair, city accent..."

"I'm here to bring him some clothes and books," Stefan explained. "Can I put the suitcase safely down here, while I say hello to him?"

"He's read the Bible from cover to cover and that's the only book in the house, so he'll be happy to see you. He's behind the barn, chopping up firewood." The farmer's wife pointed in the right direction. "Leave the suitcase. You'll find no thieves in this part of the country."

Stefan walked past the yard and the barn in the direction of the sound of an ax coming down onto wood with short, measured regularity.

Adri, who didn't see his friend approaching, worked on with aggressive energy. He was wearing some old corduroy trousers and a red checked shirt of thin flannel. He had rolled up his sleeves and his arms looked tanned from working in the sun and muscled from intense physical labor. Stefan wanted to take the ax from his hands, tear the clothes from his body and show him what it had meant to be without him all those weeks. He watched the way the ax came down one last time. The wood basket was full.

Adri turned around and his face, distorted with what Stefan saw as frustration, started to beam with joy.

"I brought you some clothes and books."

"That's nice of you." He took the basket filled with wood. "This should be enough for a couple of days."

"I saw you working. A few weeks longer without you and I would have forgotten how strong you are, how…" Stefan interrupted his own words. "Hopefully you haven't read the books I brought with me yet."

"Jakoba let you choose? Then it should be okay, you know my taste. How's she doing, and the little girl? How's everyone doing?"

Stefan was grateful for the barrage of questions. That way he didn't have to think about what they both wanted so much that it was almost tangible.

The farmer's wife was waiting with the early evening meal. Stefan had assumed that farmers didn't have to deal with limited availability of food like people in the cities and towns, but the profusion in front of him was almost painful. He saw two large loaves of bread, a knob of fresh butter, a big piece of cheese, two kinds of hard sausage, a can with ersatz coffee and one with real milk and not the watery rubbish city mothers had to give to their growing children.

"Of course we had our hot meal at noon, but I'm sure you can use a few slices of bread. Riding a bike all the way from town to here must have made you hungry." The farmer's wife invited Stefan to the table.

The others soon joined them. Adri introduced them all—the farmer and his wife, the daughter, two sons, the maid and two farmhands. The farmer led them in prayer, and out of respect, Stefan bowed his head, sending out his silent thanks to the very real people who were willing to risk everything to keep his lover safe.

After the first slice of bread, thickly layered with butter and cheese, Stefan sighed. "Even the Germans don't get to eat this well."

"They make sure they get what they want," the eldest son interrupted him. "A day or so ago we had a couple of those bastards here. Needed this, needed that..."

"They paid decently for what they bought," the farmer said calmly.

"Do you go hungry where you live?" the daughter asked.

"We're not starving, if that's what you're asking, but it's getting harder by the day for my wife to make sure our children go to bed on a full stomach. As for having a nice meal, I can't remember how long that's been." Stefan realized how his words might come across, so he hastened to add, "I don't know how my wife manages to keep us all adequately fed and clothed, but without her connections with the shop owners, trading skills and talent to make something out of nothing, we'd be so much worse off."

The farmer's wife nodded. "We're able to trade what we can't produce on the farm, bacon for tobacco, a rabbit for sugar and flour. A farmer's family never goes hungry."

Stefan tried to listen, but a foot teased insistently against his leg. He avoided Adri's gaze, but that didn't help one bit against the hardening of his cock. Soon he didn't know if he should hope for a perpetual continuation of the meal in order to avoid a potentially embarrassing situation or look forward to the farmer's closing amen after a short Bible reading.

Finally Adri said, "We have some things to discuss before Stefan returns home." Calmly he walked to the door. "We can talk in the room where I sleep."

They climbed the ladder and were alone. They undid the buttons of their clothes without saying a word, no longer willing or able to fool themselves. Adri gazed with a pensive look at Stefan's body before he said, "I want you to offer yourself to me."

Stefan didn't need any more instructions to turn his back to Adri, get on all fours and open his legs as wide as they went. He trembled in eager anticipation when his lover knelt between his thighs, spit in his hand, used his fingers to prepare the opening and pushed in. It had all been so long ago and so far away.

"You know so perfectly what I need. I'm starting to think you're able to read my mind," Adri started once they were both fully sated.

"I saw the way you were handling that wood. That told me the whole story." Stefan smiled contently. "I would be happy to bike around the world for this."

Adri fondled him like a much-loved pet. "I want to get back to town as soon as possible. The farmer and his wife have earned their seats in the front row of heaven, but except for the eldest son, there's little attraction in country life for me. I hope it'll be my turn for forged identity papers soon."

"You mean you're coming home as soon as you get the right papers? You're sure that's safe, because I can't stand to lose... Eldest son, you said?"

"A bit of a hothead, but a good bloke all in all. Willing too, I bet."

"Exactly how willing?"

"What do you think the farmer would do if he found me and his oldest son frolicking in the hay? 'Look but don't touch' it is."

Stefan frowned, perhaps because he understood his own jealousy as little as Adri's teasing. "You're your own man, if that's what's troubling you. You never made me any promises." He grabbed his clothes, but suddenly changed his mind and ordered Adri to get over onto his back and prepare himself.

"I think I'll have to make you jealous more often," Adri muttered with closed eyes.

* * * *

"You want to go back now? In the dark? Dear man, that would be a very unwise thing to do. Stay the night, and you can go back to town well rested." The farmer's wife didn't wait for a reaction, but simply herded him to a small attic room. "This should do for one night."

He was not surprised when halfway through the night the door opened and Adri stood in front of him. He made room on the narrow bed and his lover got in beside him.

"A whole night together," Adri whispered and took Stefan into his arms. "What a treat!"

"It was good, what we did earlier. Has it been enough for you?" Stefan asked, fully happy with being where he was.

"You mean to ask if we both can get hard again?" Adri's hand dipped inside Stefan's underpants to stroke the filling shaft.

The rough, but never indifferent movement of their mating gradually slowed down into a half sleep, until one of them moved again and the other reacted with a lazy smile. And suddenly there were the sounds of a working farm, right before dawn. Unwillingly they let go of each other, all too aware there was no way of knowing if and when they would ever see each other again.

The farmer's wife sent Stefan on his way with a suitcase full of cabbage, carrots, apples, cheese, sausage and a dozen eggs. "I'm sure your wife will have good use for a little bit of extra food."

Should he tell her that on the black market the cheese, sausage and eggs alone would cost more than many a worker earned in a month?

"I'm sure she will. It's very much appreciated."

* * * *

Adri got his forged identity papers and returned home, although he still needed a place to live — preferably one without a snooping landlady.

"So why don't you suggest that he rents the floor above us?" Marije, the ever-practical one, suggested. "The rooms upstairs have been empty for weeks since the neighbors moved out. I'm surprised you didn't tell Adri about it. The landlord will be pleased to earn some money with it again."

Stefan nodded, mumbling something about it being a clever idea, because what was he supposed to say to her? Should he warn her that her husband now simply had to walk up the stairs to see his male lover? She might be well aware that the anti-German resistance would be more likely to enter their house now than ever before, and she could accept it with almost nonchalant courage, but her heart was too innocent to see the other danger. She understood that suitcases with secrets would eventually bring the Germans to their door, but that didn't make any difference to her. Adri was a friend so she helped him, the same way she had helped Jakoba Huyzen after the birth of her daughter and had welcomed Stefan's mother into her home.

And Stefan felt as if he were leading a lamb to the slaughter.

Without much enthusiasm, he talked about Marije's idea with Adri.

"You want me to rent those rooms?"

"That's not a fair question, is it?"

Getting enough furniture for the three small rooms was a problem in itself, but with some asking around, a bed, a table and a few chairs could be found. Marije offered to let him share all the family meals, as long as he provided fuel and food coupons in exchange.

Chapter Twenty-Two

In his fearful imagination this had happened often enough to know exactly how to react, but in the actual moment when a fist pounded on the front door, Stefan froze in blind fear. Even the knowledge that Adri wasn't at home, that there were no strangers in the house, no suitcases, no nothing, couldn't stop the trembling of his body when he finally got up.

"Perhaps it's better to open the door. I'll go to the children to see if everything is all right," Marije told him.

Heavy boots walked up the stairs, through the rooms. Doors and drawers were opened, but not closed again. Everything was taken from its place, everything was taken into strangers' hands and dropped wherever. Even the beds were thrown over.

Stefan, his arms around Marije and the children, saw it happening. This invasion of their privacy made him silent with bewilderment, even more than it scared or angered him. A man in uniform rummaged through

Marije's clean linen, and the expression on her face pressed the last drop of blood from his heart.

Without even as much as an apology, the Germans disappeared as fast as they had entered the house.

Hours later Adri found them working ferociously to wipe out any trace of what had happened in the night. "I'm so sorry…"

Marije added more hot water to the soap mixture. "I'm out of coupons for boiled water and this is the last of my soap." She ignored Adri's apology.

"I'll make sure you get what you need," Adri promised, "even if I have to buy it on the black market with my own money."

Stefan took him aside. "We were extremely lucky you took everything out of the house a few days ago, or I don't want to know what the outcome would have been. People must have seen you coming in and out of this house for years, so I have no idea how this could have happened."

"Yeah." Adri nodded. "The fact that they haven't arrested you must mean they acted on gossip. I don't imagine for one moment they're interested in what happened back in '36."

"What?"

"The park, the kiss, the policeman?" Adri reminded him.

"I know what happened then," Stefan snapped.

"I'm sorry I mentioned it. I shouldn't have, when it's not relevant."

Stefan shrugged. "It won't matter much what we do. If they want to arrest me, they'll find an excuse. I wish I had Marije's moral courage — or yours. But I bet you're the one they were after."

"I'll disappear for a while again. If it's safe, I'll send one of the girls to let you know everything's all right."

Stefan accepted the inevitable without a protest. He said his goodbyes to his lover and greeted the heavy, sad feeling in his stomach like the return of an old friend.

* * * *

He never knew when the next message from Adri would arrive, and if it would be Trees or Truus bringing it. He just learned to trust that the next one would come. The fear of that very last message, the one he didn't want to hear? He did not dwell on that one.

On rare occasions Adri himself paid him a visit. He never stayed long and didn't say anything beyond a few platitudes in the company of Marije and the children.

"We'll play chess again," he promised Sientje.

"I bet I could beat you," the teenager said, and blushed when she realized she was bragging to her uncle, to an adult.

Adri grinned. "I'm not going to bet when I know I'll lose. But you'll have to excuse your dad and me, because we have some talking to do."

Stefan followed him upstairs to Adri's apartment. For safety's sake, his lover no longer spent the night there, but there was still a bed and a door with a lock.

He undressed, because what was the use of pretending it was about anything else? He stepped into the bed and waited until Adri joined him.

"I'm happy to be here with you. I shouldn't be, but that's how it is," Stefan sighed once he was in his lover's arms.

"Everything has changed, but not this."

"You have changed."

Adri held him tighter.

"You go from one address to the other, and even without you telling me, I know you have more than one forged identity card." Stefan struggled for words he had never needed before. "You've changed from a boy who always smiled into a man with a closed face. You've become a stranger."

"Even Marije stopped smiling."

"I'm worried, because being here is too much of a risk for you."

"If they find me, they find me. I couldn't stay away from you. When—if—I die, I don't want to have died for nothing."

How little time had passed since Stefan would have protested and told Adri he didn't want to hear the words! Now he didn't even understand why this still happened, why they were in this bed, in each other's arms. "It would be better for both of us if I made an end to this. Every time I meet you there's the risk my family will be without their provider. But I can't stop it. I'm too far gone to even know if I still love you. I…"

Adri looked at him with questioning eyes.

"I hurt from missing you." Out of words, he kissed his lover, moving his hands lower until a warm erection filled his hand. Adri did the same for him.

For a moment Stefan was at peace with his existence, but then he turned his head and saw that Adri's gun was lying on the chair by the bed.

Chapter Twenty-Three

Stefan tried to remember at what exact moment the situation had changed from merely difficult to utterly desperate, but his memory was starving as much as his body. Had they ever owned clothes suitable for the winter? Was it true that his wife and children had once sat around a table, in a heated room, each with a plate full of boiled potatoes and cabbage and gravy from last Sunday's pot roast, and perhaps even a small piece of sausage or bacon?

He came home with a few pieces of wood from one of the trees in the park. Marije, who had never before known the word for desperation, looked slowly up from her lethargic staring. "Have you brought something to eat? Do you have potatoes for the children?"

He took the decision, then and there. "It's too dangerous for the girls, with Ida being so young and Sientje looking like a young woman, but I'll take the boys to a farm — some place they still have plenty to eat.

Selle can ride his own bike, Wilfred will have to ride on the carrier of mine. Perhaps the people who took in Adri for a while last year will know a family for them. At least they'll have a chance that way."

"They're still children. They're not ready to leave their family. I'm not ready to let them go."

Selle was thirteen, Wilfred a year younger. If he stood the risk of not being there to see them grow up to be men, at least he wanted to send his sons away from a place where they would slowly die of starvation. "I don't want to see them go either, girl, but rather this than lose them to hunger or some illness. I've made up my mind. You know I've always followed your decisions regarding the children, but this time you'll have to accept I'm head of this family. Tomorrow I'll take the boys across the river. You know better than I do what to pack for them."

Without paying any attention to her sadness, he made sure she packed two small rucksacks. It wasn't nearly enough, but it was all they had.

* * * *

Just when he feared he wouldn't make it in time before the eight o'clock curfew, Stefan found himself once again in front of the door of his own home. He rang the bell for Adri's floor, hoping his friend would be home and stood motionless at the foot of the stairs with his head bowed and his hands empty.

His lover opened the door and hurried down.

"They gave me bread and potatoes and carrots and beans and even a bit of bacon," he whispered against Adri's cheek. "I carried everything past the Germans, the usual ones and even the SS, and they all said 'Walk on. Go home to your family'. When I was almost back in town, Dutch police stopped me. They took everything."

"I would have loved a nice plate of potatoes and beans, but if I really have to choose, I'd prefer to have you safe with me." Adri held him tightly.

"What am I supposed to say to Marije, to the girls?"

"Go to my floor. I'll tell Marije you're home and what happened. Tonight you're sleeping in my bed."

Stefan slowly walked up the two flights of stairs, exhausted to his bones. He stopped for a few seconds at the door of his own apartment, then climbed the remaining stairs. He sat down at the table, hiding his face in his hands. He didn't look up when Adri stood behind him.

"I'll make you some ersatz. It's not much, but it's all I've got at the moment."

Stefan didn't ask if he was drinking the last of Adri's supplies. He was cold, hungry and deeply ashamed. "I failed my family and I left my sons in the hands of strangers."

"Marije is glad you're back in one piece and the girls are asking why you don't come to see them. I told them you're very tired." Adri took Stefan's hands in his own. "We had a bit of luck today. Sientje ate with an old school friend. You probably remember Tanja, one of the Pietersens? They're up to their ears in the black market. Ida scrounged a sandwich from a German, and I found enough wood so Marije was able to cook some tulip bulbs — and you're back with us."

"Even with the boys hopefully safe and well fed, I don't know how to keep Marije and the girls alive." Stefan shook his head. "Can't they even make sure the children get one decent meal a day? They say they can't get food to the cities because the rivers are frozen and the inland ships can't move an inch, but I don't know what to think anymore. The Krauts hardly allow us to breathe, but they didn't bother me when I brought Selle and Wilfred away. They could have arrested me to work in Germany and left the boys to fend for themselves, but they didn't. But the food I tried to get to my daughters was taken away by my fellow Dutchmen. I don't understand anything anymore."

"Leave the brooding for later. Come to bed. I missed you. I have nothing to warm up the room, but we'll keep each other warm." Adri led him to the bedroom.

Under the threadbare blanket and an equally worn-out overcoat, they huddled together to find as much warmth as possible in each other's bodies.

Adri's lips hesitated over Stefan's face. "I'm sorry," he apologized. "We're both tired, dirty and hungry. This is not the time for lovemaking."

"Why not?" He was surprised at his own disappointment.

"You came home from hours of pedaling your bike on wooden tires in the freezing cold. You have nothing to show for it, except the hope that the boys will be safe. And now you want me to mount you like some animal in heat?"

"I don't know what I want. Do I have anything to want?"

Adri pulled him even closer and kissed him with a tenderness he probably hadn't felt in a long time. He made love to Stefan without hurry and almost without passion. He touched his lover's chest with gentle hands. "I can count your ribs, sweetheart. You don't even eat your own part of the soup ration. Most of what you and Marije have goes straight to the children, doesn't it?"

"They're still growing boys and girls, and I'm getting used to having an empty stomach. I would never have believed how much alike the pain of hunger and the pain of not being with you are. Now I know." Stefan touched his lover in the same way as his lover touched him, shocked by the signs of decline, but also with the gentleness of someone no longer able to see any kind of future and thus simply being happy in the moment.

"When I was riding home, I didn't think, 'I'm going back to Marije and my girls'. No, all I could think was, 'In a few hours, I'll be in the arms of my man'. My greatest fear when I was stopped by the Krauts the first time wasn't that my family would have to survive this winter without me, but never seeing you again." Stefan averted his eyes. "My thoughts should have been for my wife and children."

Gently Adri used one hand to turn Stefan's face toward him again. "You'll be ashamed of our love until the day you die. And yet you're still here."

"Don't let go of me," Stefan whispered, so softly he could hardly hear his own voice, but Adri held him safe inside the circle of his arms.

"It will be better for all of us if I leave town after the Allies have chased away the Germans. If we're still alive by that time, that is." Adri laughed without joy. "To wait every day and night until I hear your step, not knowing whether you're just saying 'hello' or have time to stay a bit longer. Without me you have a chance of returning to the normal life you've always craved. I'll just have to see how I manage as a man alone. I'm not even thirty, and there will be opportunities for me.

If it hadn't been for the war, I might have left years ago. The world is full of men, and they're not all married."

"I understand," was all Stefan could say. Exhausted to the bone, he agreed to everything he would have fought against weeks, even days, ago. Their love had failed, as every doctor and every pastor could have told them it would from the beginning. He held his lover without hope or desperation. The day of liberation would come, and if they were both alive then, it would be time to say goodbye.

* * * *

The war had been won, but the enemy refused to give up the fight. Food was on its way, the planes with flour and butter from Sweden had been the messengers of that, but for now hunger remained a heavy stone in Stefan's belly. Sharing what little food and fuel there still was proved more efficient than cooking for two households, so every night Adri ate at their table. Since the night Stefan had come back with empty hands, they had avoided each other's gaze and touches. Their friendship had finally reached the point Stefan had wished for ten years before. He was too hungry, too exhausted and too concentrated on his efforts to keep his girls alive to witness the end of the German occupation and feel any joy or sorrow. Once he did register a tender look in the man's eyes, but he no longer knew how to react and the moment passed.

His world had shrunk to the barest possible minimum. He looked for fuel and food, traded whatever their household had left after nearly five years, broke down the cupboards in his home because there was nothing left to store and burning them at least provided warmth for a few hours.

During one of his walks through town, looking for anything that could be of use while also trying to avoid German patrols still looking for halfway able-bodied men, he met Jakoba Huyzen and her little girl.

"He's been arrested. The photographer, he's been arrested." It was all she said.

Stefan nodded his concern and support, but wasn't sure if he even cared. Later he asked Adri if he knew anything of what happened to Armin.

"Do you want to hear the whole story?"

Stefan shook his head.

"A friend of a friend told me Jo Swart had died," Adri said.

"Are you sad?"

"I will be."

* * * *

The three adults and two girls had become an efficient, fully self-sufficient unit, an organism with only one purpose — to stay alive. No one left the house without a bag or sack just in case they came across anything edible, and Ida's big eyes and red hair brought her more bread from the Germans than her own parents could buy with everything they had.

Spring came, although the signs of new life remained shyly hidden. Stefan now had traded every single item his family could do without, and finally everything they still needed, but fractionally less than food. In the now practically treeless town park, he had stolen the wood from the bench Adri and he had sat on so many times. This destruction, both of one of the few beautiful parts of their neighborhood and of the place where so much of the great love of his life had been written, left him utterly cold.

With his bag of firewood, he walked home, on guard for the gangs out for everything that could be eaten, burned or traded on the black market. The Germans who remained no longer mattered, so if the soldier standing at the iron gate of the park hadn't called him by his name, Stefan would have ignored him. He turned around, but couldn't find the face in his memory.

"Stefan D-D-Doffer?" The soldier stuttered.

Achim Händler. It was as if Stefan was looking at half of a torn photo, or at a building with the façade blown away by a bomb so that the private lives of the inhabitants became embarrassingly public. "He's dead."

What was there to say? That a human being could exist between life and death without crumbling to ashes?

"How did it happen?" Stefan asked, as if it mattered.

"Someone fired a gun. He pushed me to the ground. I survived. He didn't." Achim's voice was as expressionless as his face.

Stefan suddenly felt in a panicky hurry to get away from the park. "They're waiting for me at home."

"Adri?"

"He's alive."

For a moment he imagined that the worn-out man in his worn-out uniform smelled vaguely of the man they had both known.

Chapter Twenty-Four

It was May, 1945, and the German occupation was finally over. The eagerly anticipated Canadian soldiers now filled the streets with their bright smiles and bars of chocolate. Stefan kept his promise, but his heart broke when Adri overtook him on the stairs with a Canadian soldier following in his tracks. A friendly nod was exchanged between all parties. He avoided looking into Adri's eyes.

He took Ida's hand and told her there would be music and cake and lemonade for all the children at the street party. "And in a few days I'll go and bring Selle and Wilfred home, and you'll see how fat and round they've become at the farm." He talked so he wouldn't have to hear the sorrow in his own head.

It wasn't until more than a week later that he sat across from Adri at the table. "So, you're definitely leaving?"

Adri nodded. "What other choice do I have?"

Stefan shrugged resignedly. He didn't want to ask any question that would expose how jealous and hurt he felt, but he couldn't stop himself. "Was that Canadian soldier any good in bed?"

"Which one?" If there had been the slightest hint of mockery in Adri's voice, Stefan could have hit him to express the desperation of having lost the man he loved, but it was a simple question to answer a question. "They're extremely nice, but always in bit of a hurry. I'm not the only man showing his gratitude in this way. As to whether any of them is better than you? No one will ever replace…"

There were almost ten years of memories between them. There was too much history, too much to look back on.

"You already know what you're going to do, once things calm down a bit?" Stefan talked past the moment.

"I have no idea. Move to another city. Find a job. They'll need a lot of painters and plasterers to repair the mess the Krauts have left. That's one thing that's certain."

Stefan finally gave himself permission to really look at the man sitting across the table from him. *I love you*, he thought, *now more than the first time we met. After all those years you still excite me. What of it? I don't have the courage to follow you.*

"If you need to borrow my bedroom, if you happen to meet a nice Canadian liberator, just let me know," Adri offered. "I remember how it was for us."

Stefan nodded absentmindedly. What did he care about Canadians in his bed? And what could they possibly see in him? There were plenty of young, attractive and more than willing men. Why would they even consider a husband and father, close to forty, still showing all the signs of hunger and hardship? Everything considered, how much longer would it have lasted with Adri anyway?

"Redhead…"

He looked up, saw the look in Adri's eyes and just like that first time at the bottom of the stairs, he didn't know how to react. Why, of all things, would Adri use his pet name for Stefan? Why now, when they finally had faced reality and had said their goodbyes? Since that failed trip to bring food home, months ago, they hadn't shared a bed. He had missed it, even more than he dared admit to himself. How many times had he lain next to his wife, longing to climb that flight of stairs, but remained where he was? He had controlled himself, as he would do for the rest of his life. He assumed Adri felt the same and had fully given up on their love, considering his enthusiastic involvement with the Canadian liberators.

He had been as mistaken about Adri's feelings for him as about his own for Adri. Everything was as it always had been between them, despite all their good intentions.

Adri walked to the door and up the stairs and Stefan followed, as if nothing had changed. In bed they undressed each other, experienced as the lovers they were and shy as if it were that first time, so long ago and yet so perfectly remembered.

Stefan's breath caught when his lover's cock entered him.

"I love you, love you so impossibly much," said Adri in his ear. "I can't leave you. I tried. You have to believe me. I tried and tried. No one knows how long the days and nights last when you turn your back on what you desire and the beast tears your skin apart with his claws, refusing to let go." Adri was no longer moving. "I mean every word. I want to go. I need to want that and I've tried everything to convince myself, but the thought of thirty, forty years without you makes me sick with misery. Send me away, because I can't do it on my own."

Stefan turned around and embraced Adri with a force he didn't know he still had in him.

"Here's your answer."

If he let him go he would be doing the only right thing, but the right thing would change him into a bitter man. The people with the least guilt would have to bear the brunt of his grief, cloaked in angry silence. The liberators had finally arrived, but this war wasn't over yet. One day his children would ask questions, and even though Marije would never spill the words, her eyes were messengers that his carefully hidden secret had been visible on his face for a long time. He had no choice but to accept the road that lay ahead of him.

"Sweetheart?" The voice of his lover brought him back from his thoughts. "You're sure everything is all right?"

Stefan smiled in reassurance. His past had slipped from his fingers and his future was unknown. The present was the only certainty he had left.

About the Author

In no particular order: woman, writer, in a relationship with my wife since 1981 (though we had to wait until 2001 until we could actually get married), mother of two grown sons, owner of cats (I can pretend, can't I?), reader and a lot more.

R.A. Padmos loves to hear from readers. You can find her contact information, website details and author profile page at http://www.pride-publishing.com.